To Parika,

Be sure to dog-ear the dirty parts for later reference.

Thanks for letting Joe & MaryAnn buy this for you

Hillbilly Anthology

Copyright © 2023 by Jon Ketzner

All rights reserved. No part of this book may be reproduced or transmitted in any form or by any means, electronic or mechanical, including photocopying, or recording, or by any information storage and retrieval system without written permission from publisher or author. The only exceptions are brief quotations for review or for education and information purposes by non-profit organizations.

For information address:

J2B Publishing LLC
4251 Columbia Park Road
Pomfret, MD 20657
www.J2BLLC.com

This book is set in Garamond.

ISBN: 978-1-954682-49-8

Hillbilly Anthology

Jon Ketzner

Contents

Dedication 7
Acknowledgements 7
Introduction 1
Bad Consequence for You 2
The New Kid 54
The Veronica Lake Effect 76
In the Still of the Night 106
The Ozmond Conumdrum 132
Alfa Romeo, R.I.P. 170
Ghosts of the Bloody Lane 198
Missing Linker 230
Meet the Author 263

Dedication

For Marcie, who is moderately happy that she hasn't yet joined the Widow's Club. She has always been a big fan of me doing anything with my unstructured playtime. This project kept me out of her hair during ski season. For that she is grateful; but she's not quite ready to acknowledge that mine is an important voice of our times. She'll come around.

Acknowledgements

I would like to thank Jim Brewster for his humor, encouragement, and high professionalism. He is a splendid author, editor, and publisher. To the extent that this book, such as it is, has any redeeming value, Jim is the source of that value.

I would like to also give a shout out to my crack focus group of readers and kibitzers: Marcie, Jonathan, Lacy, Jayson, Beth, Joe, Laura, Mary Ann, Val, Amanda, Debbie, Dan, Pam, Brett, Sharman, Lolita, Carol and Jim. All were lovely and encouraging, except Marcie and Carol who were harsh and snitty. And don't even get me started on Sharman. If they all buy a copy of this book, at full retail, as they have promised, the damn thing will be a blockbuster.

The cover and interior photos are by the brilliant and award-winning Dan Foye. The headshot with my bio is by the brilliant and long-suffering Marcie Grice.

Introduction

In the long ago, pre-affliction days of early 2018, my wife, Marcie, spotted an article in the Cumberland Times-News about a program sponsored by the Maryland Writers Association: Notable Authors.

Each month, the MWA selects an author (novelist, non-fiction chronicler, poet, whatever-the-hell) with Maryland roots and publishes a short biography of the author with examples of their work. This introduction to the author is sent to participating newspapers around the state, who publish the bio.

At the end of each bio, the MWA includes a "Fun With Words" challenge. Aspiring writers are invited to respond to a short prompt and write a brief (100 words) introduction to a piece inspired by the works and principal genre of the Notable Author. The prompt includes specific plot points or story elements. Selected responses are chosen by the MWA to be published in the participating newspapers.

At my wife's suggestion, I responded to these prompts. Some of my responses were lame as hell, some were encouraging. I have expanded eight of those 100-word prompts into this anthology of short stories. As MWA guru Jim Brewster likes to remind folks, "writing is fun." I hope you have a fraction of the fun reading these stories as I had writing them.

The book title "Hillbilly Anthology" is intended as a backhanded homage to the New York Times best seller and baloney sandwich "Hillbilly Elegy."

As I like to recite to my beautiful grandchildren: "I see London, I see France, J. D. Vance, Is a big poopy-pants."

Bad Consequence for You

Notable Author: Hulbert Footner (Nov 2022)

Genre: Adventure
Prompt: Using only 100 words place a character in an adventure in which they are plunged unexpectedly.

Prompt Forward

Green light. The Escalade didn't move.

"C'mon." Quinn Clark punched her horn.

The Escalade's driver door opened and a blocky, linebacker-type lumbered up.

"Now what?" Clark sighed.

The linebacker's head exploded like a melon jammed with a cherry bomb. A black Lincoln pulled aside the Escalade, two more linebackers hopped out, yanked open the Cadillac's passenger door and grabbed a screaming child. They all piled into the Lincoln and took off.

Clark peeled after them and called 911.

"Do you have an emergency?"

"You can't trace this call. You don't want to know who I am. Kidnapping at Clinton and Pine. A kid, literally. In pursuit. Call NSA. Say Bad Consequence called. I'll call back in ten. Do it now."

Click.

Chapter I -- Mexico Farms

The Lincoln scampered north on 28, exiting town across the low bridge at Whitey Ford. Then on into farm country. Clark made no attempt to disguise her intention following the kidnappers. They knew she was behind them and likely assumed she was some citizen with a misplaced sense of civic duty. They had to figure she had alerted local law enforcement to what she'd witnessed. The Lincoln's driver made no attempt to shake the tailing BMW.

Clark called 911 again.

"Do you have an emergency?"

"Know who this is?"

"Yes, Ma'am."

"You call the NSA?"

"Yes, Ma'am. They said to follow your orders. My boss needs to talk to you."

"This is Captain Jerry Fell. Who the hell are you?"

"Way above your pay grade, Captain."

"Yeah, well I got a headless corpse in the market district. And a supposed kidnapping. And every prick bureaucrat between here and Washington on my ass. And I don't like any of it."

"Yeah, Jerry, well I'm having my period and I am super bitchy right now too. The kidnappers are in a black Lincoln hauling north on 28. I'm betting they're heading towards the old grass airfield at

Mexico Farms to meet a helicopter or small plane. They know I'm on their tail. They gotta guess I called authorities. They're hauling, Jerry, but they ain't exactly hauling ass. They seem way too cool for school, Jerry. That worries me."

"So, what do you suggest, Bad Consequence, or whoever the hell you are?"

"Call the Staties. Tell them to send competent folks to the Mexico Farms field pronto. SWAT would be a good idea. I'll delay the bad guys. But I'll be expecting the calvary, Jerry, and I'll be real disappointed if they don't show. Got it?"

Click.

The Lincoln approached a blinking traffic light and turned west onto Mexico Farms Road.

"Hey, jerkweed, use your turn signal. Tool."

The old airfield was three hundred yards down the road. An ancient relic from the bi-plane days. A couple of grass runways cut at an angle in an open cornfield. No tower, just a few old metal hangars and some windsocks.

A panty blue Cessna Caravan was parked near the road, with its stairway deployed. Clark presumed the engine was not lit, but the rotating beacon and strobes were on, signaling readiness. The Lincoln pulled close to the turboprop and parked. The driver's door flew open and a linebacker got out. No sign of the other linebacker or the child.

A less blocky but obviously fit gentleman emerged from the plane. He was not wearing a jacket but was otherwise dressed in standard corporate pilot regalia. He walked calmly towards Clark who had pulled her BMW about twenty yards from the Lincoln and Cessna.

Clark tucked her SIG Sauer under her thigh and powered down her window.

At the BMW, the pilot tapped his cap and said, "Ma'am."

Clark looked at him closely and shrugged, "I called the cops."

The pilot smiled.

"I bet you did just that. Very responsible of you."

"Send the child over here. I'll take him back to the authorities. You kidnappers can beat it."

"Her. And she wasn't kidnapped. Ma'am. She was rescued by my brave associates over there. She's in much safer hands now than she would be with any 'authorities.' We and the kid will be leaving soon. Plane's turned into the wind. We're ready to go."

"I called the cops. They're on the way."

"You hear any sirens darling? I called the cops, too, and explained that it was all a misunderstanding. No one's coming. They believe the kid's in good hands. Don't you?"

"No, I don't, Sully, and I'll tell you why. Good guys don't just casually ignore a headless corpse on a downtown street and the circled W tattoo on your neck tells me all I need to know about you scumbags."

The pilot reached for the Glock stuck in the back of his pants. Before he could find his gun, Clark's SIG put a hole in his forehead the size of a fifty-cent piece. The exit wound was much messier.

Clark jumped on her accelerator and drove directly at the Lincoln. The driver had his Glock and was shooting at Clark's windshield. Bullets bounced off the shield.

"Sorry, dirtball, this Beemer has some non-standard options."

The driver reloaded. Clark swerved beside him and centered two shots into his torso. He dropped like a bag of garbage. Clark then shot the right front and rear tires of the Lincoln before spinning her car around, reloading the SIG and driving directly at the Cessna.

As with the Lincoln, she shot the plane's front landing gear tire and mechanism. She also fired six shots into the front of the plane, screwing up, she was sure, the turboprop's avionics. She didn't know if there were any other henchmen on the plane, but none appeared at the open door.

Clark turned her car to make a run back at the Lincoln. The other linebacker had exited the passenger side and was holding yet another Glock. She feared for a moment that he was going to point and shoot the little girl in the car. Instead, he put the gun in his own mouth and pulled its trigger to the expected result.

Clark pulled up aside the Lincoln and hopped out clutching the SIG. She went to the passenger door, stepping over the suicidal linebacker. She whistled.

"I guess when you work for the Wagner Group, failure is not an option."

Clark carefully peered into the Lincoln and saw a small girl, maybe six, sitting in a car seat in the rear.

"Car seat? Maybe these a-holes weren't totally awful".

The little girl's catatonic face reassured Clark that she was alive and, actually yeah, the a-holes were totally awful.

Quickly, Clark extracted the shaking child and the car seat from the Lincoln and put both into the backseat of the BMW.

"What is your name, Sweetheart?"

"Sofia"

"Do you have a last name, Sofia?" The kid just shrugged.

"Okay, Sofia, wait here. I'll be right back then we'll get you someplace nice."

No one had emerged from the Cessna. Quinn Clark approached the steps, her SIG at the ready. She climbed into the plane without confronting any more nasties with Glocks. She saw a pretty young woman, groggy and semi-alert belted into one of the dozen seats. She unbelted the woman and hoisted her into a standing position.

"Can you walk?"

"Yes. I walk. No need help." A distinctly east European accent.

The woman managed the short stairway and Clark directed her to the Beemer. As the woman passed one of the dead linebackers, she spat on the gore that recently had been his head. The young woman opened the BMW's passenger door and looked in.

"Sofia. Sofia."

"Mama."

Chapter II – Erie Waterfront

Mad Max Sokolov was not a happy camper.

"Where are those bastards?"

Colonel Maksim Sokolov commanded a cell of fifteen Wagner PMC mercenaries operating covertly in the United States. They were currently housed in a former industrial pumping house on the Lake Erie waterfront in Erie, Pennsylvania.

They'd boated from Canada three weeks prior on a clandestine mission ordered by Yevgeny Prigozin. Prigozin and Wagner had avoided operating in the United States but the prize in this assignment was worth the risk of pissing off the Americans.

Sokolov dispatched three of his best men to grab the woman and girl. They were in the Pennsylvania Amish country, for god's sake, what was taking so long? The three were ex-Russian special forces, spoke fluent American and were brutally loyal. They'd die before failing, even at their own hand if required.

The rented Cessna should have landed in DuBois four hours earlier. One of Sokolov's men was waiting there with a van to bring the five back to Erie.

Dmitri, the mission leader and pilot, reported that the grab had gone okay. The woman was snatched at an apartment, sedated and on the plane. The kid was grabbed from private security that had been hired to take her back and forth to day camp.

Ivan and Mikhail had the kid and were at the airport. They'd been followed by a nosey do-gooder. Dmitri had called a State Police captain on Wagner's payroll to shoo away any law enforcement the do-gooder may have tried to summon.

Since then, nothing.

"Call that stooge with the State cops and find out what's going on."

"Captain Bryan said to not call again, or we run the risk of burning his ass."

"Do it," screamed Sokolov.

Colonel Sokolov had earned his charming sobriquet "Mad Max" in Syria, where he was known to summarily shoot prisoners, civilians and even subordinates that riled his ire.

Fifteen minutes later, the radioman knocked on Colonel Sokolov's makeshift office door to report.

"Everything's screwed. Bryan said that a Lancaster police captain led several of his own patrol cars out to the airfield when he heard the State Police never showed. They found our three guys down and dead, their SUV and the Cessna shot to hell and no sign of the woman or the kid."

Sokolov looked at the radioman with eyes that would have terrorized Charlie Manson.

"No effing way. How is any of that possible? Dmitri and those other two were pros. No way they screw up. What does this Bryan say?"

"Well first, he's pissing himself because he's sure that he's going to get nailed for shutting down the State Police response."

Sokolov shrugged.

"Who cares? He should use his own service revolver to end his worry."

"Anyway, remember the do-gooder citizen that followed our guys to the airfield? Turns out she's a big deal at the NSA. Bryan said she is called 'Bad Consequence.' Whatever that means."

"How the hell did the NSA get on our asses? Nobody knows of this mission but our very top guys."

"Bryan said this Lancaster cop…Captain Fell… believes the woman, this NSA op, was just in town. Saw the kidnapping go down and went to war on our guys. She must have the mother and the kid. No one knows where they are or where they're going."

Sokolov kicked a trash can across the room.

"Get ahold of that NSA stooge of ours and find out anything that might help us find this Bad Consequence. And I don't care if his ass gets burned either. Make it clear that if we don't find that mother and kid, and I mean damn soon, that he'll have us to worry about, not some pussy Federal prosecutor."

"Got it, Colonel."

"And rent us another Cessna twelve-seater. Get Petrov back here from DuBois and tell those other guys to be ready to deploy stat."

Chapter III - On The Road

Once the young woman was belted in the front seat, Clark jammed the BMW and took off down Mexico Farms Road. She headed north onto 28 and drove fifteen miles then turned onto a narrow country lane heading northeast. She'd avoid any principal highway. Quinn Clark was familiar with the back country roads in this part of Pennsylvania and intended to use them to Interstate 81.

The drugged woman fell to sleep immediately, as did Sofia. Clark hadn't learned Sofia's mother's name. That could wait.

She dialed the Lancaster 911 line again.

"Do you have an emergency?"

"It's me. Let me speak to Captain Fell."

"One moment, Ma'am."

"Captain Jerry Fell."

Clark smiled.

"Do you always say your name as though it's one word? Jerryfell. You're like Liberace. It is a complete sentence, though. I like that."

"I fire jackasses for mocking my name. What's the latest on our kidnapping. Staties take over?"

"The cavalry never showed, Captain. Did you call?"

"You bet your ass I called. The regional commander. He assured me he was sending warriors asap, including SWAT. "

"Well, apparently, Russian mercenaries have more sway with the State Police than you do, Captain. They were able to call off the rescue. If I were you, I'd take some of my own folks and hustle out to the Mexico Farms airstrip and lock down that scene before other folks on a Russian payroll get there and sanitize it. "

"We'll roll as soon as this call is over."

"You're going to find three deceased bad boys and a mortally wounded SUV and Cessna."

"You killed a Cessna?"

"My bad."

"Where do you want to meet to pick up the kid?"

"I got the kid and her mother, who'd also been grabbed. I'll keep them for a while until I suss this out."

"Bring 'em in. We'll protect 'em. None of my department is working for the Russians, I can assure you."

"I'm sure your team is clean. But this little kidnapping seems to have gone international. No offense."

Click.

Clark stopped at a Kohl's near Hazelton. She woke the sleeping woman and asked her shoe size, and that of her daughter. She told the woman to stay in the Beemer. Locked, it was impregnable. She bought several practical outfits for both mother and child.

Clark thought to herself, "I kinda like buying kids' clothes."

A few hours later, the woman awoke and then Sofia.

"Mama, I'm hungry."

"We stop soon, Sofia. Eat." She looked at Clark expectantly.

"Sure, we need gas anyway."

South of Scranton, in the fading sunlight, they pulled off 81 into a Wawa. The woman, Clark now knew her name to be Maria, and Sofia went into the convenience store to get food and snacks and breakfast supplies.

As Quinn Clark pumped fuel, Sofia came out of the Wawa and stood watching Clark.

Two large Harley-Davidsons pulled aside the next fueling island. Clark gave a quick look, noticed the grizzly drivers wearing Satan's Apostles regalia.

Clark thought, "Whatever."

Clark heard Sofia squeak "Ow," and turned to see one of the motorcyclists gripping the little girl's shoulder.

"Hey, kid, you're momma's a piece of ass. Maybe you'll grow up to be a nice piece yourself."

Clark looked at the biker.

"Yo, Fatboy! Take your mitt off that child."

He released Sofia. She ran over to her mother, who'd just come from the Wawa.

"Well, now, that's her momma. And damn if she ain't quite a piece herself. A whole damn family of fine tail. Maybe you'd like me to put my mitts on you."

With that the dumbass reached his paw towards Clark.

Clark intercepted his gloved hand with her own and quickly pressed his fingers back to his wrist. The inverted digits made a satisfying snapping sound. The biker screamed, "Son-of-a-..." and started dropping to the ground. As his hefty torso was sinking, Clark's booted foot accelerated upwards catching the Apostle pointblank in his little apostle. Again, the impact sound was most gratifying.

With his wingman writhing on the ground, the other biker came towards Clark.

"You stupid bitch."

Clark rapid-fired a left-right chop combination to his exposed throat. Down he dropped and, like his buddy, was impaled by a well targeted boot. He landed on his fellow Apostle. They both lay moaning and vomiting.

Quinn Clark took the SIG from the door compartment and screwed on a custom suppressor. The two bikers watched her and gurgled in panic. She waved the gun in their direction then put two quick shots into each of the Harleys.

Clark returned the gun to the door, took the fueling nozzle from the BMW and secured the cap. She walked over to Maria and Sofia. She knelt and cupped Sofia small face in her hand.

"I will never let anyone hurt you. Do you understand me?"

Sofia nodded.

"Do you believe me?"

Sofia stepped from her mother and wrapped her short arms around Clark's neck. Clark looked up at Maria, who had glistening tears in her eyes.

"Do you believe me?"

Maria managed a small smile.

"Alright, then, let's go to a nice place. A safe place."

Maria and Sofia returned to the car. Clark stepped into the driver's seat. She looked at the still blubbering, puking bikers, lying atop one another.

"You boys enjoy your honeymoon."

Chapter IV – Erie Waterfront

Radio operator Kournikova knocked on Colonel Sokolov's office and entered when told. Mad Max was in a high bad temper.

"Tell me something I want to hear, Kournikova."

"Our guy in the NSA, who is pissing his pants, said almost all intel on this Bad Consequence woman is buried deep in their files. Their covert ops are well hidden. The NSA is supposed to be just a bunch of math nerds. All wet work is way off the books, and this woman is super-secret."

"C'mon Kournikova, quit teasing me. Unzip my pants."

"Like I said, our guy is pissin but he did as deep a dive as he could. He didn't get much. He found some ten-year-old construction bills, tagged to this Bad Consequence, for work done on a cabin in eastern Pennsylvania. Area called Poconos. Town of Skytop."

Sokolov word searched Skytop and located a small town about 30 miles east of Scranton.

"Does that NSA asshat think this is where the woman took our ladies?"

"He doesn't know. His best guess. Says operatives like this woman have unlimited resources. If she built a safehouse in this Skytop, it's probably a hard target, half fortress, half arsenal."

"Do we have assets nearby?"

"No Wagner assets. Russian bad boys have a big footprint in Scranton. Those guys will take orders from Wagner. They'll do whatever you want. Chief thug there is some cue ball, gym rat named Alexi Rozin. Should I call him?"

"Now, goddamnit."

Five minutes later, Mad Max was chatting with a very solicitous Alexi Rozin.

"What can I do for you, Colonel?"

"I need three helicopters, mid-sized, immediately. Bell Rangers, something like that. Can you make that happen?"

"Probably. We have a chump here in town who runs an air tour business, flies over the Poconos and out towards the Pennsylvania Grand Canyon. Likes gambling and friendly ladies so we own him."

"Find a private landing strip near Wilkes-Barre Scranton Airport that can handle small Cessnas. Deliver the copters there. Our guys will pilot. We'll be there in a few hours. Got it?"

"Yes. Do you need any other help? Some bandidos or muscle? Weapons?"

"We got all we need. Your blundering goons are not, shall we say, as nuanced as this mission requires. We'll meet you at the air strip. Bring the keys for the choppers. Then you can go back to your…enterprises."

Rozin extended his middle finger at the phone.

"I got it, Colonel. See you soon."

Sokolov told Kournikova to load the Cessna and prep the men. He wanted to fly out of Erie "not just effing yesterday, but effing day-before-yesterday."

Chapter V – Skytop

Quinn Clark had the three-bedroom, log home built on a pastured hillside outside Skytop. Using NSA "miscellaneous expenditure" funds, she had the home built woodside, with significant excavation into the mountainside. The underground structures included a large safe apartment, stocked with survival foods, water and oxygen.

The bunker had its own water and electricity, powered by batteries and solar panels tucked miles away. The water came from an underground spring. A small escape tube hidden behind a pantry led to an old coal mine shaft and eventually to the other side of the mountain.

The bunker was hardened against anything less than a small nuclear device. A two-foot thick, impenetrable vault door was controlled by a biometric lock keyed to Clark's voice, fingerprint, and retina.

Two smaller hardened bunkers, also built into the mountainside, contained an impressive array of weapons and small ordinance. The woods behind the house included four layers of the most advanced high-tensile wire security fencing snaking through the trees. The third layer was lethally electrified and controlled at the bunker.

Clark had posted between the fencing and the house, a series of heavily disguised hunting stands that offered clear sight lines at the large meadow in front of the house. The property and surrounds were blanketed with small cameras, motion monitors and more than a few remotely armed personnel mines.

The log home was very comfortable, decorated in an understated wood and fabric motif. High powered computer and communication technology, driven by several redundant sources, were in the house and the safe bunker. Clark could Sat call anyone in the world, or link with pretty much any computer system anywhere, including China or Russia. Quinn Clark had built similar redoubts in Sedona, Japan, Australia and two in Europe. All courtesy of the NSA's office supplies and management budget.

Late in the evening of the kidnapping, Clark and her two guests pulled into the garage under the log home. She closed the reinforced garage door. Inside the garage was another super modified BMW and a silver, tricked-out Ducati motorcycle.

Clark showed Maria her room and Sophia's. They both retired immediately. Clark armed the extensive security system, checked a spate of urgent messages from Derek at the NSA, ignored them and turned in.

Chapter VI – The Visitors

Next morning, Quinn Clark sat on the deck, sipping an espresso, and looking over the pond in front and the meadow in front of that. The meadow was large. It ran from one steep cliffside to another, and down several hundred yards to the long driveway from the country road to the house.

Clark thought the Skytop setup was tippin-toppin. Now that she had brought outsiders, though, she would need to abandon this safehouse and build a new one on the east coast. Maybe down outside Lexington, Virginia. Good thing the NSA has deep pockets.

Maria and Sofia came onto the deck. Clark put breakfast food in the kitchen and Maria fed herself and her child and brewed her own espresso. Self-sufficient guests are the best.

Sofia, seeing the pond, looked expectantly at her mother.

"You can play there but be careful. Don't fall in." Sofia skipped down the steps.

Clark appraised Maria, who, showered and scrubbed, was lovely. The clothes from Kohls, on Maria, looked like Paris fashion.

"So, Maria, before you tell me what the hell is going on. What is your last name?"

"Yurigar. I am Maria Yurigar."

"And Sofia is Sofia Yurigar?"

"No, that is not it. Her name, as you say, is what the hell is going on. She is Sofia Zelensky."

"Like the Ukrainian President? That kind of Zelensky? Is she related to President Zelensky?"

"She is the daughter of Volodymyr Zelensky. That is why Russian bastards want her. And me."

Clark processed the news. Now, much of what had transpired made some sense.

"Maria, does President Zelensky know he has a daughter here in America."

"No. He knows nothing of Sofia. He and I...we met on his program. He and Olena were separated. He was fun guy. We hung out. I got pregnant but did not tell. Then he went back to Olena."

Maria sipped her espresso.

"I have a rich uncle...you would call him oligarch...he paid for me to come to America. Have child here. Make citizen."

Clark looked at Maria and smiled, "Uncle?"

For the first time, Maria laughed.

"Yes. He real uncle. Good uncle. Decent uncle. He pay for us to live quietly in Pennsylvania farm country. Like where I grew up. He pay for everything."

Maria watched her daughter stare intently into the pond.

"He pay for Sofia to go to camp. She is smart. He even pay for driver to take her. Joseph. I fear now that Joseph is dead."

Clark nodded. Maybe if he hadn't gotten out of his car to come give Clark a piece of his mind at the stop light, he'd still have all the pieces of his mind. Probably not.

"Does your uncle know about Sofia's father?"

"I never told. I'm sure he know. Baby papers say Yurigar, not Zelensky. My uncle make sure we are hard to find. If he know, he never tell Russian bastards. He live in London."

"Well, somebody figured it. Then sicced the Wagner goons on you and Sofia. You two would make quite a prize and bargaining chip for the Russians."

Clark thought but did not say, "and it would probably end very badly for both of you."

"You think Wagner coming to kill Sofia and me?"

"Actually, I'm sure they want you alive. Dead, you're not much use to them. You're both safe here."

Maria smiled.

"We know we are safe. Sofia thinks you are Wonder Woman. She said she loves you. Thank you for being so splendid. Thank you."

Clark smiled and nodded.

"Yeah, well, I better go check in with the folks who are paying for our little vacation."

Maria nodded and walked down to join Sofia by the pond.

Clark went to her office and called Derek on her NSA security phone.

"Holy crap, BC, what the hell is going on up there? Kidnapping, dead Wagner guys with your signature written all over their cadavers. Crazy local law enforcement types screaming at us and each other. What's going on dude?"

Clark told Derek most of it, excluding the Zelensky tie-in and where they were.

"Derek, everything else is way above your pay grade and security clearance. I need you to patch me in to General Nakioma pronto."

"You think I can just get the NSA Director to take my call, then your call?"

"I know you can Derek. You're brilliant. Make it happen asap. Tell the Director that Bad Consequence needs to talk to him, Code Unitas."

"Can you tell me whatever the hell that means?"

"I'd have to kill you. Make the call happen now, Derek."

Click.

As Clark hung up, Sofia came in. She spotted the teak, in-laid chess table and hand carved wooden chess set next to Clark's desk.

Sofia looked at Clark, "What is your name?"

"My name is Bethquinn Clark."

Sofia nodded and returned her gaze to the chess set.

Clark smiled. "So, Sofia, do you play chess?"

"A little." A barely there squeak.

"Do you want to play a game with me?"

A shy nod.

Clark told Sofia to play white and move first. Sofia trapped Clark in a fool's mate in four moves.

Clark looked at Sofia.

"Damn girl, I thought I was a cold-blooded killer."

Sofia grinned.

"Alright you little prodigy. Set 'em up again."

Clark hung around a bit longer the second game but was soon mated. They played three more games. Sofia cleaned Clark's clock each time. Clark's security phone beeped.

"Thank God. Sofia, I gotta take this call. Go find your mama. You can kick my ass some more after lunch."

Sofia grinned once more, hugged Clark, and skipped out of the office.

Clark pushed the green button. "Talk to me Derek."

"Okay, BC, I got General Nakioma on the line. He seems pretty pissed. Might be missing a tee time or something."

"Piss on him. Put him through. And thanks, Derek."

"Always a pleasure, BC."

Chapter VII – General Peter Nakioma, Director NSA

"Good morning, General."

"Ah, the famously lethal Bad Consequence. A pleasure to finally make your acquaintance."

"Actually, General, we have crossed paths before. I knew who you were. You did not know me. I like to keep things compartmentalized like that."

"Well, now that's worrisome. The NSA's deadliest assassin within striking distance of whacking me and I had no idea."

"If I was going to 'whack' you, you would most assuredly not see me coming. No worries, though, I have no assignment file on you. At the present time."

"Good to know. Okay, you Unitas my ass. What's so damn important?"

Clark reviewed the previous day's events, this time including the Zelensky information. But, again, not revealing where they were safe-housing.

"Based on one easy to buy tattoo, and the word of a stripper who probably pissed off her Cartel boyfriend over a custody battle, you want me to do what?"

"General, you have a nest of Wagner vipers operating in this country right now. These guys are definitely Wagner, not just some Russian Mafia types. Mobsters don't reach for their Glocks just because someone identifies one of their tattoos. They sure as hell don't blow their own heads off rather than report disappointing news back to their boss. The woman, Maria, might be a stripper…I didn't ask her, she's pretty enough…but I do believe her story. These Wagner jackals sure believe it."

"So, again BC…can I call you BC?…what do you want from me.?"

"Put out an APB on the Wagners. There's a cell someplace, within a Cessna ride from central Pennsylvania. They're here, which should alarm all your national security bozos."

Clark shook her fist and continued.

"And you should tell the Secretary of State, or better the President, to alert Zelensky to what's going on so he can plan his response should the Russians threaten to execute Zelensky's six-year-old daughter on YouTube if Ukraine doesn't stand down."

"Well, I'll tell you what this bozo is going to do. I'll have our smarty-pants analysts look for any suspicious and recent Wagner-like activities in the Mid-Atlantic region. If they're here, we'll spot 'em. But I sure as hell am not taking any of this to State or, for godssake, the President."

"I hate these guys." Clark hissed.

General Nakioma droned on.

"I don't know where you got the woman and kid stashed and I'm sure you won't tell me. I know your insubordinate record. You bring them into an NSA safehouse in Jersey or New York and we'll sort this out."

"Find and neutralize the Wagners, General. I'll take care of Maria and Sofia."   Click.

Chapter VII   Scranton

About the same time Quinn Clark was concluding her unsatisfactory conversation with General Nakioma, a rented Cessna Caravan landed at a private airfield near the Scranton Wilkes-Barre International Airport.

Colonel Sokolov was the first down the short stairway. He was greeted on the tarmac by a large bald man in an ill-fitting sport coat: Alexi Rozin.

Sokolov thought, "I hope this meat locker isn't as stupid as he looks."

"Ah Colonel Sokolov. At last, I meet the legend. I know we will be fast friends. May I call you Mad Max?"

Kournikova, who had followed Sokolov down the stairs, visibly flinched.

"You may not ass wipe."

Rozin stammered. He was not used to getting alpha-maled in his own backyard.

"Sorry, Colonel. The helicopters you requested are ready."

The three Bell Jet Rangers were old but seemed well maintained. Grice Tours was decaled on the side of each.

"Are you sure, Colonel, you won't need pilots for these birds, or at least local navigators."

"We'll manage. Do you have accommodations for our fifteen?"

"I count just twelve, sir."

For not the first time, Solokov had forgotten he lost three men at the Battle of Mexico Farms.

"Twelve then. Do you have adequate accommodations for my men?"

"Yes sir. We have ten rooms and five baths in an apartment building we control in downtown Scranton. Not far from the steam museum." Rozin grinned like an idiot.

Solokov stared at Rozin as though he was looking at a large pile of elephant dung.

"Fine. Let's get going."

Once settled in their rooms and having sent Rozin away with a dismissive wave, Solokov called his men together in his apartment, the largest.

"Tomorrow, Kournikova and Mikhail will fly one of the helicopters to Skytop and reconnoiter this bitch's safe house. They will take videos and photos."

Mad Max brushed something from his shoulder.

"Moscow is supposed to be sending us satellite shots as soon as they can reconfigure some orbits. Fools. We brought a couple of drones which we can use for reconnaissance. Mostly, we want to determine if the targets are there and their level of protection."

Kournikova asked, "What if they are not there?"

Sokolov's face turned grim.

"Then we will go to Ft. Meade and get that NSA puke and use our own enhanced interrogation techniques to force him to tell us if the NSA has them and where they are."

The Colonel spit on the floor.

"Hopefully, this Bad Consequence cowgirl is keeping them safe from her own idiots and making our task easier."

Solokov looked at his men. He busted their balls but he loved them all. They were Mother Russia's finest: deadly, ruthless, and completely loyal to him.

"Get some rest. When Kournikova and Mikhail get back tomorrow, we'll make our plans. I want to be out of this manure pile in two days, three maximum."

Nods of agreement from the mercenaries. This place was getting hot.

"Don't drink until the mission is complete. That idiot Rozin has some ladies' downstairs…plump Belarusian girls…if you need to scratch that itch. But no vodka. I will see you tomorrow."

Next day, Kournikova and Mikhail returned to the airport. Mikhail had flown a Bell before. They flew east. Kournikova had no trouble finding the log house outside the small hamlet of Skytop. The copter circled the property several times, trying to appear a tourist ride showing some fat Americans the beauty of the Poconos.

They spotted two women and a small child strolling and playing around a tiny pond. They photographed and videoed extensively, capturing the details of the house, the nearby woods, and the large meadow in front. On their fifth sweep, Kournikova saw that the shorter women was staring at them with what looked like very sophisticated binoculars.

Kournikova felt a chill of fear. He never felt that.

"Let's go Mikhail. We are pressing our luck here."

They returned to Scranton.

Chapter IX – Daddy

Quinn Clark waited two days after speaking to General Nakioma before hearing again from the NSA. She and Maria and the child spent those days resting, de-stresssing from the harrowing kidnapping and rescue. Maria joined Clark in her yoga and workout in the small but full gym. Maria was quite fit, but could not keep up with Clark's regimen.

"You are strong lady, Wonder Woman. You could beat anybody."

"I'll tell you what, I can't beat that kid of yours in chess. Damn, she's a steely-eyed chess assassin."

"She is very smart. Genius, maybe. My uncle wants her to go to private school in Delaware. Very exclusive. Academy. Very expensive. Uncle says, no problem. That's what Sofia deserves. I worry though."

Sofia and Maria enjoyed being outside the log house. The weather was cool. The leaves had not changed. But the Poconos were as lovely as advertised in "Bride Magazine." During that first day of R and R, Clark noticed a small helicopter flying nearby. It stayed at altitude, but kept returning.

With her Sunagor Mega binoculars, Clark scoped the helicopter. Look like a typical tourist copter. Two passengers, both male. The bird hovered for one more moment then took off west. It did not return that day or the next.

Clark checked Grice Tours on the internet. Seemed legit. Small operation out of Scranton. She called but got a recorded message saying they were closed for several days handling a special private occasion. She did not mention the flyovers to Marie.

Near noon on the third day, Clark took a secure call from the NSA.

"Hello, Derek, what's shakin?"

"Hi, BC. Got some news, some of it might be troubling."

"Go ahead."

"Well, as ever, you were right. We back traced a ton of intel that when regressed with your info, we believe, are sure, we found where your Wagner boys came in and hung out. They have been hunting and prepping from an abandoned building in the old GE Diesel works in Erie. Came from Canada on small boats. Took off before our guys stormed the place. Been gone at least two days."

"Go on, Derek. Get to the troubling part."

"So, we believe, are sure, that they flew out of Erie on a rented Cessna. They put in flight plans for Chattanooga, but never arrived there. We think they probably landed at a small airfield somewhere like the Mexico Farms strip. Could be anywhere within 1000 miles of Erie."

"Got it. What else?"

Well, here's what's troubling. As we cross-referenced all this, we picked up an unauthorized search inside our own files. Someone with high clearance had taken a sudden interest in one Bad Consequence. Your files are purged except for some old innocuous invoices. Construction company crap not sufficiently buried in the off-budget stuff.

"Who's the NSA person looking for my info?"

"We don't know yet. Someone high up, someone who knows the system, someone who knows how to cover their tracks. But he or she is one bright person against 500 bright people. They'll be exposed. "

"You gotta mole there, Derek."

"Yeah, we know. One last thing, we're pretty sure this Wagner cell is no more than eighteen mercenaries and we believe their commander is Colonel Maksim Solokov."

"'Mad Max.' Sent the A team. Okay, then Derek, I need for you to patch the President of Ukraine through to my SatCom, full audio and video. ASAP."

"You want me to turn water into wine, BC, while I'm at it?"

"You the Man, tiger. If anyone in this world can make that happen, it's Badass Derek. Life and death, big boy. I'm pretty sure Mad Max is right around the corner. Saw some suspicious air recon the other day."

Clark rubbed her eyes and looked at her chessboard.

"Do your magic. Again, ASAP. If Zelensky's security push back, say the request is from Bad Consequence, Code Brady. And don't ask. I still don't want to have to kill you."

Click.

Clark found Maria and Sofia who were eating lunch.

"Hey, ladies, stay in the house and close by. I'm going to need you both in my office. I hope soon."

It was soon. Twenty minutes later, Clark's lap-top pinged and Derek appeared.

"Okay, boss, I got 'em. They initially told me I was crazy. But I mentioned you and the Brady thing, bada-bing. When I punch off, you'll be looking at President Zelensky at his undisclosed location, and he at you at your undisclosed location. I love this spy stuff. Good luck."

Clark recognized Zelensky. Not just from his being a media mega presence. She stood three feet from him in Kyiv back in 2019, on a clandestine protection assignment during the impeachment nonsense. He would not remember.

"Good, evening, Mr. President. Thank you for speaking with me. I hope I am not interrupting your dinner. If you prefer to speak Russian, I can manage."

"Ah, Miss Bad Consequence, this is a pleasure. English is fine. My Security Chief assures me that he can protect me from any assassin…car bomb, GRU, James Bond…but if Bad Consequence comes looking for me, I am a dead man walking. I very much want to be your pal."

"You are the world's pal, Mr. President. My great honor to chat with you. I won't take much of your time. I know you have a rat extermination project on your hands. First, I would like you to meet a very good friend of mine."

Clark waved Sofia to come climb on her lap.

"Mr. President, this is Sofia. Sofia, say, 'hello.'"

"Hello." Sofia smiled and waved.

"Hello, child. You are a very pretty little girl. I hope you are behaving for this nice lady who holds you now."

Sofia quick turned to smile at Clark, then said to the monitor, "She is Wonder Woman. I love her."

Clark smiled. "Do you know this little angel, Mr. President?"

"Alas, no. She is lovely. She reminds me of my little Oleksandra when she was that age."

"Well, sir, that is not a coincidence. Sisters tend to resemble one another." Clark waved to Maria to come sit next to her.

Zelensky sat back and asked "What do you mean? Sisters?"

When Maria sat down, she spoke to the monitor, "Hello Volodymyr." She smiled warmly.

"My god, Maria, is that you? Are you in America? Is this child yours?"

"She is ours, Volodymyr. And we are in big danger. We would be kidnapped or worse had not this brave woman rescued us."

Clark recounted the events of the last several days. Zelensky sat in silence. He listened intently while staring closely at Sofia.

"Mr. President, we are dropping much on your already overcrowded plate. It would be natural for you to have doubts about Sofia's paternity. I can assure you Wagner has no doubts. Mad Max has no doubts. They will do anything to get Sofia and Maria and then use them against you and Ukraine."

Zelensky sat for a moment, cleared his throat, and then wiped an eye with his hand.

"I, too, have no doubts that I am at last meeting my beautiful daughter. This war has brought me many unhappy moments. This evening has brought me great joy."

Clark smiled at Sofia.

"And thank you Miss Bad Consequence for guarding my precious Sofia and my lovely Maria. How can I help you?"

"Thank you, Mr. President. I have spoken to the Director of the NSA about this situation. He is skeptical and wants this to be handled bureaucratically. That strikes me as most dangerous. He refuses to alert higher-ups as to the great risks to Sofia and Maria and, frankly, you sir. "

"Bureaucrats, they are the same the world over." Zelensky groaned.

"What I would ask you, sir, is that you use your juice in Washington. Call our President directly, if you can, and ask that he intervene to bring Sofia and Maria to safety."

Clark stared hard at Zelensky.

"Sofia was born here. She is an American. Even if you are not her father, the President should help rescue a little six-year-old American from these Wagner bastards."

"I will use all my, as you say, juice to help you protect these precious ladies. Immediately."

"Thank you, sir, you are a man of honor and decisiveness. I must go now to prepare for some uninvited visitors. I guarantee you that Sofia and Maria will not be taken by those Wagner pricks. I will leave you to share some private words. It has been a pleasure, Mr. President."

"No, thank you, Miss Wonder Woman. You have my unending respect and gratitude."

Chapter X – Checkmate

Clark assumed that Mad Max used the info from the NSA mole to know where they were. His Grice Tours reconnaissance alerted him that just the three were at the safehouse. She was confident they would not attack at night. Too much uncertainty about defensive positions and booby-traps. They would approach from the front, across the meadow and early in the morning to ensure as long a day lit battle window as possible.

The big question was when they'd storm the log house. Solokov probably knows from his mole that the NSA is alerted to the Wagner presence in the United States but has not yet gone into a high defense readiness condition. He'll want to get this done and be gone before the Feds go all DEFCON 1 on his ass. Which means the attack will most likely begin the next morning.

After dinner, Clark moved Maria and Sofia into the hardened bunker. She pointed out the supplies and the hidden escape tunnel. She recalibrated the biometric lock on the vault door to both Maria's and Sofia's voices, fingerprints, and retinas.

"You will be safe here. It would take them a month to get into this bunker. At most, they would have a few hours to try. I don't intend to let them have even that."

Quinn Clark pointed at an illuminated monitor.

"Do not open that door until President Zelensky pops on that screen and tells you it is safe to do so. If you never hear from him, wait two weeks, and push that f5 button. That will connect you to Derek at NSA and he'll help you. That fails, use the tunnel. Climb down to the road, flag a ride, and work your way to a town. Call your uncle in London. There is plenty of cash in that drawer. I'm sure that President Zelensky will be calling in an all clear soon, probably tomorrow."

Sofia's face was small and worried.

"What about you? Won't you be coming back?"

Clark softly cupped Sofia's face.

"I get to have all the fun, Sweetie. I am going to do to those bad men what you do to my chessmen. Checkmate. I'll see you again. I love you."

Sofia hugged Clark around the neck.

"I'll be brave like you, Bethquinn."

Clark smiled. She so seldom heard her name.

Maria quietly hugged Clark, smiled bravely and locked the vault door after Bad Consequence stepped out to rain hell down upon Mad Max and his band of murderous men.

The sun peeked over the Poconos the next morning. A black SUV parked at the bottom of the meadow on the one lane road that led to the log house.

"The Russians are coming, the Russians are coming," mused Clark.

She was perched in the northern most camouflaged deer stand, cradling a tricked-out Barrett M82, with a custom suppressor and Vortex scope.

The SUV was too far away for Clark to take a credible shot. She waited. A man in black stepped from the Ute and opened the trunk. He handed something to the driver.

Clark heard the buzzing sound of two drones flying above the meadow towards the house. She zeroed each and shot both from the air with her suppressed sniper rifle.

In the SUV, Colonel Solokov hissed, "What the …?"

Clark smiled. She figured Mad Max was in that vehicle and was going to command the assault from well behind battle lines, getting a drone's eye view of the action.

"You'll just have to follow the game on the radio, Maxie boy."

The game was about to begin. Three small Grice Tours helicopters popped over the western ridge and landed well down the meadow. They probably intended to land closer to the house but had been warned about the drone kills. Instead, they would proceed uphill through a long meadow, directly at a sniper armed and dangerous and Ruskie hunting. Bummer.

Ten mercenaries, in full infantry regalia including body armor, piled out of the copters and got low. Clark figured the car held two more bad boys.

"Damn, just twelve. You guys are ridiculously confident. I was hoping for a more target rich dawn hunt."

The ten separated into standard battle formation and began advancing up the meadowed hillside. They kept low. Quinn Clark thought the .338 caliber anti-material ammo she was using would pierce the Wagner body armor. But to be sure she intended to go for head shots.

Two unlucky bastards on the south side of the formation were not staying low enough for their own good. In quick succession, Clark fired two skull shots, exploding the mercenaries' craniums like grapes macerated under a Tuscan maiden's pretty toes.

While Clark's rifle and ammo were designed to suppress sound, no high-powered shot is silent. The remaining mercenaries were pros and flashed scopes from their low squats in the general direction of Clark's perch. Time to move.

Bad Consequence slid down and sprinted past the second and on to the third, mid-south stand. She was fully camouflaged and confident she was invisible among the trees. She had pre-positioned a Barrett and ammo at each of the four stands.

From her new angle, Clark enjoyed a better vantage for henchman hunting. She quickly waxed two more Wagners who were keeping their heads well down but were more exposed to her new perch. The remaining six quickly swung in her rough direction.

Down the meadow, the other two exited the SUV and approached. They each shouldered long range RPG launchers and their dead reckoning was directly at Clark.

She jumped this time from the stand, tumble-rolled into a dash and ran like hell towards the southernmost stand. The RPGs hit north of her previous stand, effectively destroying it, as Clark dove into the forest floor.

"Damn, those pricks brought RPGs to a gunfight."

Clark waited from her new position. Colonel Sokolov and the other dude had joined the surviving six brigands. All were hunkered and waiting. They were not sure if the RPGs had taken out the sniper. They would wait. As would Clark.

Occasionally, one would raise a headless helmet slightly trying to draw Clark's fire. They had seen too many movies. She did not take the bait.

Clark's SatCom pinged with a message. She clicked a GPS signal and waited. One hour later, the Wagners gauged that the sniper was down. All eight low crouched toward the house. Clark let them go.

Colonel Solokov and his men slow crawled through the meadow, around the pond, then triple-timed to the garage, maintaining standard close and cover protocols. Kournikova used a small explosive device to open the door. The surviving Wagners ran into the garage, past the two BMWs and on into the house. They needed another forty minutes to search the house.

"They're not here, Colonel."

"Of course they are, you moron. That murderous bitch built this fortress. She figured they would be safer here than anywhere on the road. The woman and kid are here and hiding."

Mikhail called from the garage. All ran to join him. He had lifted a hinged pegboard from the mountainside of the garage. Behind the pegboard disguise was a formidable steel door with a biometric lock.

"They are behind that door! Kournikova, can you open that damn door?"

Kournikova studied the door, whistling appreciatively.

"I don't know, Colonel, maybe if we had plenty of time. I can't tell how thick that vault door is, but I'm betting two feet, and I-beamed into even thicker concrete."

The mercenary shrugged. "Comrade Putin wishes he had such a door on his Armageddon bunker."

Solokov looked at his watch. "You have ninety minutes."

The other men eyeballed Kournikova. His expression said it all. "I will try, Colonel."

Colonel Solokov's SatCom phone chirped. Nobody could reach him, only Wagner Chairman Prigozhin.

" Yes, Yevgeny, we are very close."

"Sorry Mad Max...can I call you Mad? This isn't that prick Prigozhin." Whoever it was mispronounced the prick's name.

"Who is this?"

"Why, this is the President of the United States. I've been watching your 'Dirty Dozen' show here in the situation room in the White House. President Zelensky is watching too from Ukraine. He agrees it's great television, and he should know."

"Bastards." Solokov had noticed all the security cameras.

"Your guy couldn't open that door with a small hydrogen bomb. You should also know that, like Putin, I ordered a special military operation. You probably hear the copters landing outside. These are real copters...Apaches and Chinooks, not cute tour helicopters."

The President's voice grew harsh.

"When you step outside, you'll be greeted by about 200 deadly and pissed Special Forces. I would recommend surrendering. If you boys would rather die for Mother Russia, they'll be glad to accommodate you. One last thing, jackass, I will not forget or forgive that you Wagner bastards came to the United States to kidnap a six-year-old American citizen."

Mikhail peeked out the damaged garage door and confirmed that an army was out there, locked and loaded.

Sokolov quickly figured on a prisoner swap somewhere down the line for himself. He ordered his men to stand down and surrender.

What the Colonel and the other mercenaries did not anticipate, as they were perp marched to a waiting Chinook, was Mad Max Solokov's head exploding like a grape macerated under the pretty toes of a Tuscan maiden. The shot apparently came from the south.

The American commander was under Presidential orders to ignore any such incident and he righteously followed those orders.

Epilogue

President Zelensky appeared on the bunker's monitor smiling and told Maria and Sofia they were safe and to open the vault door and greet Colonel Chamberlain, the American commander. Once among the soldiers, they both looked for the woman who rescued them. Maria noticed the Ducati motorcycle was gone and was not surprised that Wonder Woman was gone too. That she entered their lives was an accident, a miracle, for which she and Sofia would forever thank God.

They moved into a small house on Dover Air Force base where Sofia became a big hit, especially among the Base's chess club members. President Zelensky very publicly acknowledged Sofia and thanked the President, the American military, and an angel for rescuing Sofia and Maria.

Mrs. Zelensky was thrilled to have a new family member and gracious and kind towards Maria. The Zelensky children welcomed a baby sister and could not wait to meet her.

The Wagner Group and the Kremlin denied any responsibility. Western lies and misinformation, except for the part about Zelensky being a shameless womanizer and fornicator.

Six months after the events in Pennsylvania, Sofia celebrated her seventh birthday at the Milford Academy for Gifted Children in Delaware. Her mother was there, along with Maria's new fiancé, a Navy Seal she'd met in the Poconos. Among Sofia's birthday presents were a big box of gifts from her new family in Ukraine and a model of Air Force One from the President.

She also opened a beautiful mahogany box with the hand carved chess pieces from the Skytop log house. With the chess set was a Wonder Woman birthday card. Printed inside was a note:

"Happy Birthday my little, ruthless chess assassin. I miss you and your mama. Be Happy and know that I will never let anybody harm you. Never... BC."

The New Kid

Notable Author: Colby Rodowsky (Jan 2021)

Genre: Young Adult
Prompt: Write no more than 100 words about a young adult going through tough times with the help of an understanding adult and include an attic or a library

Prompt Forward

First day, first class at Parktown Day School and transfer student Conor Del Santo struggled understanding Mr. Kelso's trigonometry lecture. Conor asked a question on similar triangles which his teacher answered.

Then Mr. Kelso asked the entire class, "Any more stupid questions?"

His new classmates' roaring laughter drummed Conor's ears.

Later, at his library study hall, Dr. Fritz greeted Conor and asked about his first day. Bob Fritz was chairman of the Parktown math department and knew that Conor had just moved to Seattle from New York. Conor reluctantly recounted his humiliating first period.

"I guess I'm too dumb for here."

Second day, first period and Conor saw Bob Fritz standing at the board. Dr. Fritz asked everyone to sit.

"Mr. Kelso is no longer at Parktown. I'll be subbing until your new teacher is assigned. Alas, there are stupid people...teachers even...but in this class, I can assure you there are no stupid questions. Got it?"

Chapter 1: Conor Del Santo

After that first day, Conor settled into a normal routine. Transferring as a senior was tough. Moving from Manhattan to Seattle, though, was fine. Conor liked the area. He was shy…lower spectrum shy… but he was not without confidence in certain things. Math and girls, to the contrary notwithstanding.

Parktown was private. Conor had always attended private schools. His father, who Conor didn't see often, was wealthy and he and his mother were comfortable. He knew his way around the treacherous waters of teen snobbery and snottery. Generally, he stood to the side, engaged with his fellow students as little as possible and privately enjoyed his music and games and solo explorations of his new hometown.

Conor transferred in early November, well after the clubs and cliques of Senior society had been established. Other students were looking forward to the three P's: Preparing college applications, proms, and partying. The college thing was under control and Conor wasn't a prom or party guy. He was a good-looking kid, with exceptional eye-hand coordination and could've played sports and been successful in that silly high school jock way. None of that was important to him.

Girls noticed Conor and flirted with him good naturedly. One co-ed smiled.

"Hey, Del Santo, thanks for getting Kelso's ass kicked out of here. What a jerk."

While Conor did not necessarily think that was one of his best moments, he grinned and shrugged, "You're welcome."

Lory Del Santo, Conor's doting mother, encouraged him to try and enjoy his last year in high school. She urged him to look into the music department, she'd heard it was quite good at Parktown, find a best friend and, maybe, a girlfriend. Conor would just roll his eyes at every suggestion.

"I know you like girls and I bet they like you. Lord knows your Daddy sure was and is catnip for the ladies." Conor would just give his "whatever" shrug.

One day, to get his mom to back off a little, he told her, "Okay, I'll check out the music stuff. Now can you just stand down?

Lory smiled and said no more.

Chapter 2: Pop, Rock, and Jazz Club

Conor met with his guidance counselor to review his first few weeks at Parktown. Conor's grandfather once told Conor that "those who can, do; those who can't, teach; and those who can't teach, are guidance counselors." But Mr. Daisy was an okay guy. Eccentric but well-meaning.

Mr. Daisy always re-introduced himself to Conor as though they were just meeting.

"Hiya, Conor, I am Paul Daisy, your counselor."

Mr. Daisy would say his name in one word: Pauldaisy, like a disease or something. Generally, Parktown students referred to him as Paldazy. If Mr. Daisy noticed or was upset by that, he never expressed any annoyance.

"So, Conor, how is the newest member of the Class of 2004 assimilating?"

"Fine, sir. No big hassles. It's not my first time to the rodeo. I've transferred schools before. I'm fine."

"Well, most of your fellow seniors are working on SATs, college apps, essays, and references. You told me before you have that under control. That right?"

"Yeah, I'm good. But I was wondering what extra-curricular music activities are available to a late arriver like me?"

"Hmm, let's see, Conor. We have a fine student orchestra that can probably find a spot for you even if all you can play is a whistle. There's a full chorus which will make room too, even if you can't sing a lick. There are some smaller choral groups, but they require some singing skill. "

Conor had no interest in the orchestra. He sang fine but he wasn't a chorus guy. "That it?" he asked Paldazy.

"Conor, we do have a Pop, Rock and Jazz Club which is hard core and hard-wired right now. They tend to be the best musicians in the school. Very competitive."

Conor looked interested but kept still.

"And the Club itself competes. Seriously. We're very proud of them. They've finished second in the Seattle Area Popular Music Competition in the last three years. We always finish right behind those bastards from The Park School. Excuse my French."

Conor grinned. "So how do I check this Club out?"

"Okay, well the Club is led by Dr. Dent, who is super enthusiastic, over caffeinated and kinda fierce.. They practice every day in Studio B off the auditorium. The SAMPC is coming up in a few weeks. In fact, it's the day after our Senior Prom. I'm sure Dr. Dent would let you watch a rehearsal."

Mr. Daisy shrugged at Conor and continued.

"But to be honest with you, I doubt that you can join the Club at this late date. Check it out. At worst, you'll hear some good music. That whistle spot will still be open in the orchestra."

After school, Conor found his way to Studio B, heard musicians tuning, playing a few bars of familiar songs and some nice vocals. He slipped himself into the room quietly and sat down, unnoticed.

The Club consisted of a lead guitarist, two keyboardists, a saxophonist, a drummer, and a male and female vocalist. The singer, one of the keyboardists and the drummer were girls. Conor had previously noticed the singer and thought she was cute. He knew from one of their joint classes that she was, like him, a Senior.

The Club rehearsed in earnest, trying to master the George Harrison tune "While My Guitar Gently Weeps." Clark found that amusing. The two vocalists and the drummer, who was mic-ed, sang fine, but with little energy. This drove the young faculty conductor...Dr. Dent, I presume...to great exasperation.

"C'mon, guys, you're singing like cadavers. Man, we only have a couple weeks. This is our big kill shot. We need this."

Dr. Dent nodded to the guitarist.

"Okay, Grantland, why don't you jump on the bridge. Maybe that'll goose the vocals."

The guitarist, Grantland, who had been accompanying the vocals with a light hand, stood, and started burning the song's guitar bridge solo. He was good. Harrison would've appreciated his tight riffs.

Grantland was a handsome fellow, more man than boy, and seemed pleased with himself. Conor had noticed him around school too and assumed he was the quarterback on the football team. Mr. Daisy said this Club was held in higher esteem around Parktown than the football squad. Grantland was clearly the alpha stud in this huddle.

After Grantland's hot solo, Dr. Dent called it a day. Conor heard Grantland say something to the vocalist, Lolita.

"Ah, yes, Lolita," thought Conor.

Dr. Dent noticed Conor.

"Hello, son, you here from the school paper? You lost? You a spy for The Park School."

"No, sir, just interested in the Club. They're good. Nice harmonizing, blending, transitioning."

"Ah, a music scholar. What do you think?"

"I think you need to reinforce your rhythm section. Your lead guitarist is fine, great, but you need more horsepower underneath. That would help kick the vocalists in their...double sharps."

"Very astute, young man...we had a pretty good upright bass player until last week. He ran afoul of the school's pharmaceutical policies and no longer matriculates at Parktown. "

Dr. Dent wearily shrugged his shoulders.

"The bass players in the orchestra are, to put it diplomatically, god awful. So we're going commando back there."

"Well, you still sound pretty good."

"Pretty good isn't going to get it done. You don't happen to play a double bass upright?"

"Sorry, sir, no."

"Well, you have a good ear. Thanks for stopping by."

"I don't have an upright, but I do have and play bass guitar. I could bring it around tomorrow and maybe sit-in and see if I can help."

Dr. Dent looked at Conor appraisingly.

"You're that new kid that got Kelso chucked, aren't you. What a tool. Him not you. So, you missed our tryouts. Yeah, come back tomorrow, we'll see what you got. It's your funeral."

Chapter 3: The Tryout

The next afternoon, Conor strolled into Studio B carrying his bass guitar case. Dr. Dent introduced him to the ensemble.

The female vocalist, Lolita, grinned.

"Oh, I know you. Hope you can play, we need you."

Conor was introduced to Grantland.

"You're a very good guitarist."

"I know. Are you any good?"

Conor chuckled and shrugged. He set up behind the keyboardists.

Dr. Dent noticed his guitar. "Holy crap, Conor, is that a Hofner 500?"

"Ah, yeah. I got this for my birthday a few years ago from one of my dad's pals."

"Well, damn, damn boy. I hope your playing is worthy of that battle axe. Do you need to warm up? You want us to play something first till you get a feel."

"Not necessary, Doctor. Let's jump on 'Weep.' Key of C-major, right?"

Grantland snorted, "Well, hello, Buddy Guy."

"I'm just the bass player. Why don't you take us out?"

Dr. Dent frowned, "I'm the boss around here. One, two three..."

The instrumental intro was much fuller. Conor clearly had a great ear and sensed exactly where the combo was going without having to read the charts. His playing technique was superb.

The two vocalists looked at each other and grinned. They started singing ("I look at you all/ See the love there that's sleeping/ While my guitar gently weeps"). Their take on the song was rich and emotive. Grantland's bridge and final instrumental solos were great. He killed. They all killed.

Nobody wanted the song to end. When Dr. Dent waved them to close.

"I'll be damned. Die Park School. Die."

The entire combo, even Grantland turned and applauded Conor. Lolita grinned.

"Del Santo, you passed the audition."

Dr. Dent scuttled rehearsing "Weeps" more that afternoon. He didn't want to ruin the vibe. Instead they'd practice the two vocals that would complete their competitive program.

Lolita and the other singer, a good-looking kid named Vincent, would open singing Leonard Cohen's "Hallelujah" as a duet. Lolita would follow with a solo performance of Etta James' "At Last." The Club's set would finish with the kill shot "Weeps."

Lolita and Vincent harmonized fine on "Hallelujah." The instrumentation was strong, and Conor found a soulful bass groove quickly. They would grow into that tune. It would be a strong opening for them.

The combo could not get their playing or vocals around "At Last." Grantland said, after their fifth false start, "that's a turd."

He was right. Lolita's reading was rote and uninteresting. Conor saw she had the chops. But "At Last" was wrong for her. Great song. Fine singer. But no chemistry between the two.

Dr. Dent called it a day.

"No rehearsal tomorrow. See you Thursday. Fine job, Conor."

Lolita stepped over to Conor.

"Damn boy, you're 'mazing. You may have saved us."

Conor grinned. "Thanks for letting me in."

"No, you're great. I suck. That's my damn song...I love Etta James...I just can't nail it. I'm going to screw our chances."

"Are you and Dr. Dent married to that song?"

"Well, probably. He thought I made a good choice. It's a great song."

"Look, if you bought a great pair of shoes but when you got 'em home they didn't fit, that doesn't mean they're not great shoes. They just don't fit you. "At Last" just doesn't fit you."

"I love all my shoes, even if they kill my feet."

Conor looked at Lolita's smiling face. She was lovely.

"Could you trust me to help you? No other agenda, I swear."

"Maybe I want you to have an agenda," she smiled shyly.

Conor sat back. "Um, I thought you and Vincent were probably a thing."

Lolita giggled. "You and Vincent are more likely to be a thing."

"Oh, oops. He's a good-looking dude but not my type."

"I'm not really with anybody. I told Grantland I'd go to the prom with him. He's been after me to go out with him for a while. So finally, I agreed to the prom. But he's not my type either."

Lolita grinned at Connor.

"Getting back to your original question, I do trust you to help me with my performance. You're definitely a funky monkey."

Conor wrote "I'd Rather Go Blind" on a note card.

"Do you know this song?"

"Not really. Maybe."

"Pop your buds and listen to this song 10 or 20 times. Pretend your gut and vocal cords have ears. Make them listen too. I know you've had training. Breathing is good but you want to find this in here."

Conor almost tapped Lolita's chest. She smiled at his goofiness.

He coughed, "Okay. Tomorrow."

Chapter 4: Etta Girl, Lolita

Conor waited in Studio B the next day. Lolita came in smiling.

"Conor, you are so right. This song is the one I should be doing. I listened to it like you said. I will make it my bitch."

"Great. Now you sound like Grantland."

Conor smiled and waved his hand.

"Okay, I put a mic by the keyboard. Sit next to me and let's make this bitch your bitch."

Conor played a low organ melody. Lolita was impressed that his musicianship was so comprehensive. She sang to his accompaniment and her style was very close to Etta's. She loved how it made her feel.

She asked Conor, "So what do you think?"

"As Grantland would say, that's a turd." Conor ducked her punch.

"No, obviously, this is the Etta James song for you. I'll make new charts for everyone tonight and then we'll sell it to Dr. Dent and the others tomorrow."

Lolita had been around music trainers for most of her life, but this Conor dude was high torque.

"My one suggestion…order, really…is that you bring more rasp, more vocal fry to that middle eight. You got it. I've heard it in there trying to get out. Go drink a gallon of whiskey or smoke a carton of cigarettes. "

Conor smiled at Lolita. She leaned over and kissed him.

"Thank you," was all he could say.

"We need to concentrate on the competition but maybe afterwards, we could like, you know, like hang out."

Lolita grinned.

"That would be nice. I was wondering, where are you going to college next year?"

Conor shrugged, "I've already committed to Berklee in Boston. How about you?"

"Wow, you've already been accepted to Berklee. Wow. I'm hoping to get into Chapman. "

"You should apply to Berklee, or Julliard. You're plenty good enough."

"You sound like Paldazy."

"Well, he's right."

Conor realized he'd been holding Lolita's hand the entire time. He looked at her.

"Don't go to the Prom with Grantland. Go with me."

"Nah, I already promised. It'll be quite platonic, I assure you." She giggled.

"It better. Be careful. You know how guitarists are."

"I'll wait for your slow hand." More giggles.

"Well, I would rather go blind girl than see you with Grant-land."

Lolita kissed Conor again.

"You need to work on that vocal fry."

Chapter 5: Die. Park School. Die

As Conor and his folks were ready to leave for the 2004 Seattle Area Popular Music Competition, his phone rang. Lolita, sniffing.

"Hey, Lolita, what's the matter? What's going on?"

"Oh, Conor, everything's crap. Grantland, that ass, and Vincent are both out. We'll have to drop out of the competition today. It's terrible and it's all my fault."

"C'mon Lolita, what happen?"

"Well, you know I went to the Prom with Grantland last night."

"Yep. I spent the night trying to go blind."

"This isn't funny. Anyway, when we got to the Prom, he starts trying to kiss and grope me. He said disgusting things to me about wanting a little down payment on the after-Prom fun."

Lolita catches her breath.

"As if. I opened the door to get out and run away, and he came flying around the car to grab me again. "

"The bastard."

"Well, then, Vincent and his date show up. Vincent came to help me and Grantland punched him in the throat."

His throat. Punched his throat. Damn.

"His date, who is captain of the gymnastics team ran over. Grantland then punched that kid in the head. Grantland broke three fingers doing that. The gymnastics guy punched Grantland in the gut and he puked all over his tux and my shoes. Dick!"

"Crap. You okay?"

"Yeah, fine. But Grantland and Vincent are both in the hospital. Dr. Dent already said Grantland's out of the Club and probably out of Parktown. What a mess."

"Now what?"

"Dr. Dent still wants us all to meet at the Convention Center. The whole school will probably be there. Anyway, I guess he's going to tell us we must withdraw. I should have gone to the Prom with you. It's all my fault."

"It's not your fault that Grantland Lassen is an asshat. Keep the faith."

Conor had already put his bass guitar in the car but told his mother that he needed one other thing. They drove to the Convention Center.

Backstage, Dr. Dent explained the situation to the families and other Club members.

"Unfortunately, we must drop out of this year's competition. Which is terrible for our twelfth graders."

Lolita sobbed next to her parents.

Connor approached Dr. Dent.

"Doctor, we don't have to drop out. I can sing and play lead guitar. We won't have a bass guitar, but we've been there before. Adrenalin will make up for that. We can do this."

Dr. Dent smiled at Conor.

"Buddy, I appreciate your moxie. You probably are a fine singer. But you haven't rehearsed and how are you going to manage the "Weeps" solos? You're a bass player."

A voice behind Dr. Dent chimed in a deep British accent.

"Oh, mate, he can handle it all. Trust me."

Dr. Dent turned to face a couple of, he assumed, parents. Conor introduced, "These are my folks Lory and Eric."

While Conor pulled a guitar from his case, Dr. Dent stared at Conor's dad.

"Eric? Are you the Eric I think that you are?"

"Probably. And that's my boy who I love dearly. And who has more musical ability in his little toe than I have in my whole grizzled body."

Eric punched Conor's shoulder.

"And don't you worry about those solos. That little red Gibson Conor is holding burns that tune. George gave that to me. I taught it everything I know."

Dr. Dent looked at Conor with his red Les Paul and saw the fearsome angel of reckoning coming for The Park School.

He looked back at Conor's smiling dad.

"Thank you, Mr. Clapton. We got to go kick some Park School ass and we'll meet you back here with a trophy."

And they did and they did.

Afterward, Dr. Dent clapped Conor on his back and spoke to Conor's pop.

"Eric, I believe your boy makes that guitar weep better that you."

Eric smiled and hugged Conor.

"He does bring heavenly tears to my eyes."

Epilogue

This story takes place in a parallel universe.

In 1991, Eric Clapton's son, four-year-old Conor, tragically fell 50 stories to his death after a cleaning lady failed to properly shut a window. His mother Lory said, "He loved listening to his father's music and had dreams of being like Mr. 'Slow Hand.' I understand every kid wants to do what the father does, but in this particular case, he really wanted it very badly."

Clapton's song "Tears in Heaven" was written for Conor. He also played, unaccredited, the lead guitar on the Beatles' recording of "While My Guitar Gently Weeps."

The Veronica Lake Effect

Notable Author: Dashiell Hammett (Sept 2019)

Genre: Hard-Boiled Crime
Prompt: Using just 100 words, write Hard-Boiled Crime that takes place in San Francisco in 1929. Name your Private Eye, pick and include a San Francisco street and landmark, and describe the pending crime and victim.

Prompt Forward

She slipped into my office. I thought, "God, I'm giving you a big 'atta-boy' on this one."

Lithe, honey-blonde hair, more curves than Lombard Street but dressed like Pacific Heights. "Mr. Arch?"

The frosted door on my one roomer read "Jack Arch Investigations." Normally, I would've cracked wise at the obvious. But her legs convinced me to just nod.

"Mr. Arch, I need your help. I'm Valerie Garrett. My husband lost everything in last week's crash. I think he's going to shoot me for some insurance money."

She said this, tapping her bosom.

"Lucky bullet," I thought.

Chapter I -- Valerie Garrett

I gestured to a wooden hardback chair by my desk. She sat lightly and crossed one nyloned perfection over another as the hem of her violet dress slid northwards. More impure thoughts to confess to Father Carter next Saturday.

Without speaking, Mrs. Garrett extracted an onyx cigarette case from her purse, opened it and demurely plucked a Lucky Strike. She looked at me and cocked an amused eyebrow. I couldn't tell if she was asking permission to smoke or telling me to piss off if I objected. I nodded and lit the coffin nail with my desk lighter. She blew a lucky cloud of carcinogens my way.

"As I was saying, Mr. Arch..."

"Call me Jack," I finally spoke.

"As I was saying, Jack...I am dreadfully fearful that my husband, Carson Garrett, intends to kill me. I've seen the insurance applications."

Dreadfully fearful.

"Mrs. Garrett, how do you think I can help you?" She made no offer to call her Valerie or Val or V.

"I'll give you one thousand dollars. You're a private dick. You must be a tough guy. You look like a tough guy. Go have a mean chat with Carson. Tell the bastard you know what he's up to."

Another delighted Lucky Strike plume wafted my way.

"Warn him off. Threaten him if anything happens to me, you'll make sure his ass fries, one way or the other."

I smiled. "You're kidding right?"

"I sure as hell am not kidding. I know that slimeball. I can tell you're a hound dog like most men...nothing wrong with that...and when you look at me you think I look like a million bucks."

She paused for affect and recrossed those perfect gams.

"When Carson looks at me, he literally sees a million bucks. And he wants it. The cash, not me."

Well, if nothing else, Valerie Garrett was an astute judge of character. She had me figured as a hound dog and I wasn't even dry humping her shapely leg. Yet. I sighed.

"Look, Mrs. Garrett, in my racket sometimes you got to muscle up and get wet and dirty. Sometimes, rarely, I carry a gun. Mostly, I track down bill skippers, horny husbands and stupid teenagers who think they can become movie stars."

I gave her my best ex-cop deadpan.

"If I look like a rough guy that's because my mother was homely as hell. I don't do strong arm stuff. Sorry."

She glared at me. "Well...Jack...do you know anybody in your racket who is not as precious as you? Some guys with balls?"

I did know some guys like that...plenty of guys like that...and they would eat her like a cheese sandwich.

"I'll tell you what, Mrs. Garrett, you give me three hundred dollars and I'll noodle around your husband and see if something's hinky.

If I smell some sewage, we can discuss any further services you might require."

She pursed those naughty red lips and gave me a look.

"Okay, but I want a receipt. I want a detailed accounting of this noodling around. I might look like a dumb blonde, but I can assure you, Mr. Arch, that I am not stupid."

"A receipt and a full written report are all part of the service."

She took a fat gob of twenties from her purse, peeled off fifteen and slid them onto my desk. I wrote a receipt. She gave me her telephone number and address.

We both stood. She offered a finely manicured, delicate hand for me to shake.

"Thank you, Mr. Arch, when can I expect to hear from you?"

I shrugged. I had nothing else on my dance card.

"A couple of days, tops."

She gave me a flash smile, turned, and slipped from my office. I watched her retreating dorsal. Father Carter was in for a treat next Saturday.

Chapter II -- Thom Wheeler

I called Thom Wheeler and asked was he free for lunch. He was and invited me to join him at the Yale Club at 12:45.

Thomas B. Wheeler and I went back to junior high school. Thomas Wheeler or Thommy Wheeler or Thom Wheeler or ThBW...always with the "h"...was the alpha male at Braddock Junior Senior High School. He was not the smartest kid in school, or the best looking or the finest athlete but the teachers thought him brilliant, the girls adored him and he captained any team he joined.

In every aspect of teenage existence, Thom Wheeler was smooth as a milkshake. Early on he adopted me as his senior deputy. He said I was a rude and crude dude and he liked that. His proximity and validation made my high school years terrific.

After graduation, Thom Wheeler married and quickly impregnated the prettiest girl in the class. They soon crashed and burned. He graduated from business school, then law school. He was a partner at Jeffries-Lazard by thirty. He formed his own firm, ThBW, providing high priced advice on all matters to a select clientele.

He's never been too swell to get together with his old rude and crude dude paison Jack Arch. Thom's toothy grin was as sharp and genuine as the crisp miniature herringbone pattern in his blue linen suit.

"Jackie-boy, how ya doing?"

"Hey, Thom, you know you don't always have to meet me at one of your clubs for lunch. I can buy you a burger someplace, especially if I invite you."

Thom nodded. "No problem at all, big boy. Lunch is a small price to pay for some of your outstanding tales of gumshoe adventures."

He then looked into my eyes and said, "You saved my life back then. You know you did. I'll owe you forever. Besides, you're great company."

Wheeler swept his arm around.

"All these pompous asses would love to be having lunch with me. You're better than any of them. I mean that, Jack. Enjoy your Yale Club burger."

"Well, thanks, Thom. You're a good friend and you owe me nothing more than that friendship." We chatted about old buddies and his estranged son and ate our lunch.

"So, Thom, do you know a character named Carson Garrett?"

"The real estate guy? I've met him. Why?"

"Just doing some gum-shoeing. What's your take on Garrett?"

"He's nothing special. Has a real estate investment and management shop down on Grant. The Garrett Group or Garrett Enterprises or some such. I guess he makes a living. He's one of those guys with store bought hair and probably wears a corset."

Thom's grin turned, no other word for it, wolfish.

"His wife is a piece of... well, she's a piece of everything, mostly a piece of work. They kinda hang on the fringe of local swellness, more wannabes than actually-ares."

I nodded, played with my burger.

"I've met the tempting Mrs. Garrett. Did Garrett get damaged in some recent crash, something that would make him desperate for money?"

"There's been no crashes lately, that I know of. His type are always desperate for money, for cash. Let me ask around and I'll give you whatever I hear. "

"Thanks, Thom, for not making me ask you to do that."

"No probs, big boy. I like gum-shoeing myself. I'll call you if I catch anything."

"Thanks, Thom."

Chapter III -- Carson Garrett

Next morning, I sat in my Ford, sipping coffee, and private-eyed Garrett Properties, Inc. The firm occupied a faux-Tutor office building on Grant Street, close to the main financial district. The building was good-sized, owned by Garrett Properties and its only tenant.

I watched a couple dozen employees enter the building. About 9am, a new Cadillac parked directly in front and a lumpy fella with suspicious hair hauled his lumpiness out of the Caddy and went into the building. Carson Garrett.

Faithfully, I noted the impressive census of employees and the prosperous appearance of the firm. I wrote down Garrett's license number and even snapped some Kodaks. No detective purpose really, other than to sandbag my final report to the fair Mrs. Garrett. Got to earn those three hundred smackers.

At 10:15, Carson Garrett came out, hopped into the Cadillac, and started down Grant.

I whooped.

Hoping he was headed for a girlfriend or a boyfriend or an insurance office, I followed the flashy Cadillac. I tailed him discreetly in my nondescript Ford. What a pro.

We jumped on the thruway, crossed the bridge, and drove into Oakland. I followed Garrett into a dodgy commercial area of diners, dry cleaners, fortune tellers, shoe shops and bail bondsmen. Garrett parked in front of a vacant storefront with a Garrett Properties sign in the window. He sat in his car.

I parked a block away, grabbed a newspaper I keep for just these purposes, walked back towards Garrett's position. From a bench behind the Caddy on the other side of the street, I pretended to read the six-month-old newspaper.

Didn't wait long. Soon, a sleek roadster pulled in behind Garrett and a very dapper fella bounced out while Garrett lumbered from his car. The new fella was not only very dapper, but he was also very familiar.

"Oh, for chrissakes, Thom, what the hell are you doing?"

Carson Garrett was clearly delighted to see Thom, shook his hand profusely and made a grand gesture towards the sad, empty storefront. Garrett fumbled with a big keyring, found the right one, and he and Thom disappeared into the building.

I hustled to my car and reapproached the building, pulling to the curb just as Thom and Garrett came out. Garrett was still gesturing with his arms like a monkey on cocaine, patting Thom's back and grinning idiotically.

They shook hands and Thom bolted in his roadster. Garrett, still grinning, locked the building, got into the Cadillac, and headed towards Frisco. I followed him, wondering still what the hell Thom was up to.

Garrett drove to his office, parked in his anointed spot out front. He did not enter the office but walked two blocks down Grant and ducked into a tidy white building. A red awning and a sign announced the Princess Restaurant.

I parked, grabbed my ancient newspaper, and entered the Princess. Carson Garrett was jammed into a window booth, still smiling, studying a menu. I perched at the counter, ordered coffee, and observed Garrett closely.

He sure seemed plenty harmless. His toupee was good quality but obvious to anyone observant. The booth was small so his gut cantilevered onto the table. Guess Thom wasn't corset worthy.

Garrett's face was whiskey blotchy but not terribly so. His fingers were manicured, his clothes off-the-rack though probably a Magnin's rack. Carson Garrett was a burgher from central casting. But a wife killer? Unlikely.

Valerie Garrett wanted me to have a mean sit-down with her hubby---scare him off his murderous plotting. I've talked mean to bad boys in my day, and I've been mean talked to by some others. Generally, it doesn't work.

Redding up on someone either elevates their testosterone to a level of fierce resistance or makes someone feign compliance then come back at you crazy and suicidal. In my experience, war is not the failure of diplomacy. Diplomacy is a weapon of war.

"Screw it."

I picked up my newspaper, sidled to Garrett's table and slid in across from him.

"Afternoon, Carson. How's the tuna melt?"

He looked at me blankly. Up close, his whiskey blotch was more pronounced.

"Do I know you?"

I handed him a wrinkled business card (I'm waiting for some replacements).

"Jack Arch Investigations? Again, do I know you?"

"We've not met before Carson. Your wife hired me."

His expression morphed from blank to dumb.

"Valerie hired you. For what? She want a divorce?"

How the hell did this guy ever woo Valerie into a marriage bed? My mind's eye could not stop seeing the two of them taking a bubble bath together. It's unnatural.

"Mrs. Garrett's convinced you plan to kill her to collect some insurance money. She wants me to suggest to you that would not be a terrific idea."

"She wanted it to be a strong suggestion." She said "mean." Piss on it.

Carson Garrett's blotchy, burgher face slowly migrated from dumb to downright festive. His eyes twinkled like a deranged Macy's Santa and his slivery lips curled into a rictus maw. He cackled so loud the other lunchers looked our way.

"Hey, Sherlock, which Val came to see you? Slinky, sultry Veronica Lake Val or wholesome, girl-next-door June Allyson Val?"

The little bald, pudge-bucket was enjoying himself.

"Looking at you, obviously a lug who thinks with his little head, I bet she shimmied into your office, or garage, or whatever dump as Veronica Lake Val."

The prick smacked the table, scaring the hell out of his tuna melt.

"She sells that Veronica Lake pretty good. I sometimes ask for Veronica on our anniversary or my birthday. The only thing more entertaining is you interrupting my lunch to try and tough guy me. What a putz."

I should have stayed at the lunch counter and gotten a piece of pie. In for a dime, in for a half-quid.

"Chuckle all you want porkchop, but you've been warned. Anything untoward happens to the missus, I'm going to take it personal."

Garrett pulled himself up to his full real estate semi-tycoon height and growled, going all Cagney on my keester.

"Listen, dick, my insane wife has been telling folks for years that I plan to kill her. She's crazy. Nuts. But you know what? I'm crazy nuts for her and we get along just fine."

He then cocked his head and pointed a chubby finger at my face.

"I don't know how much of my money that crazy bitch gave you. I don't care. But if I ever see you hanging around me or her again, I will slap the pricks from Whitefield, Mason, and Green Attorneys-at-friggin-Law on your dumbass so fast, you'll think you're back in a prison shower. Got it, tough guy? And get some decent business cards."

Carson Garrett shoe-horned his pudginess out of the booth and marched out of the Princess Restaurant with his dignity intact. Unlike, say, me.

Chapter IV — Jack Arch

After losing the Battle of the Princess Restaurant to that bewigged butterball, I moseyed over to the nearby Landis Business Supplies to raise exaggerated hell about my tardy business cards. I was feeling a little homicidal myself and took it out on poor Mr. Landis. He promised the cards and my stationery would be delivered pronto. I grabbed some other items and took off.

Still not having lunched, I spent one of Mrs. Garrett's bucks and bought two tacos from a street guy in Union Square. I reviewed the whole Garrett matter and laughed at my silly, pathetic self.

"Some skirt shows up in your office Arch, and you shift your brain straight into jackass gear. You are a putz. Garrett has you pegged."

With nothing better to do and feeling vaguely annoyed, I drove to Pacific Heights to check out the Garrett digs. Veronica Lake Val had given me her address.

The Garrett home was a handsome stone structure, with carefully manicured landscaping. Wasn't the biggest home in the neighborhood of big homes. But it wasn't the smallest one either.

A familiar jazzy roadster was parked on Garrett's small circular driveway.

"Oh, sweet Jesus, Wheeler. Now what are you up to?"

If I knew Thom, and I sure as hell did, he would be taking an early afternoon dip in Veronica Lake. The bastard did not bother to discreetly park around the corner.

Once again, my buddy got first dibs. All I was getting out of this little episode was humiliation, three hundred bucks and, maybe someday soon, new business cards. I drove away.

Later, I did some big league drinking near City Lights and returned home late that night. I slept alone and not well.

The next morning, after breakfast, in my apartment building basement, I burnt old files and rags in the furnace. I don't like tossing old case files and the super is fine with me using the furnace to incinerate them.

I took a drive north of the city to clear my head and to mentally pre-draft my report for Valerie Garrett; always the professional. By the time I returned to Frisco, I was pretty sure Mrs. Garrett was not going to be pleased with my services. C'est la vie.

My office door was open and Brian, our doorman, was placing a large box and some mail on my desk. The return label on the box identified the sender as Landis Business Supplies. Finally, the stationery, envelopes, and fresh business cards. I pulled my pocketknife to slice open the box. The phone rang.

"Arch."

"Hey, Jackson." My childhood pal, Thomas Wheeler.

"Hey TBW."

"Don't forget the 'h,' Jack. I checked out this Garrett guy. Even met him and pretended to be interested in one of his raggedy-ass properties."

"No kidding, Thom. You did that?"

"Yeah. Been gum-shoeing my ass off. I might take it up some day if I get tired of being rich."

I waited. Thom seldom needed prompting.

"Anyway, the guy's as dull as Tuesday night. But he's legit. Doesn't have eff-you money but he's more than comfortable."

I said, "Got it."

"He doesn't need any insurance money. If his wife was a nagging porker, he might want to whack her. But this tool's bride is so out of his league, it's nuts. Have you met her, Jack?"

"You know I have."

"Well, there you go. I love me those vanilla wafers. Anyway, that's my report. Hope it helps."

"Thanks, Thom. Catch you on the rebound."

My mail was a phone bill, an Aimee Semple McPherson flier, and a thank you note from a widow who needed my help getting her late husband's money from a shady savings and loan. No checks or money orders.

I sliced open the box with my pocketknife. The first thing I noticed was wax paper which seemed odd. The second thing I saw was matted hair, the honey strawberried by blood. Gods of blood. I did not have to see her face to know whose head was on my desk.

I fumbled for the phone and dialed my old number at SFPD Central. When the desk Sergeant answered, I screamed like Fay Wray.

Chapter V -- Detective Larry Brady

San Francisco's finest were at my office in minutes. They arrived in waves, loud and conspicuous. In that short interlude between my call and their cacophonous arrival, I floor sat in the corner of my office and drank two large Dixie Cups of Canadian Club. Hiram Walker is a great pal when a bodiless woman drops over.

"Hey, Mrs. Garrett," I burped to the box on my desk, "Okay to call you Valerie now?"

The bull in charge was Chief of Detectives Larry Brady. We'd been at the Academy together. Big solid guy, good cop, mostly honest cop, not too stupid but Cal Tech was never going to miss him.

Brady said his own name as one word: Larrybrady. Which was what he was called by the other cops behind his back. "Chief Detective Brady" in front of his front. He was a detective legend at the precinct. Larrybrady always gets his man.

"Hey Jack. You seem to have a woman's head on your desk."

"Thanks, Larry, for the info."

"You know her? Tight date wouldn't put out?"

"I know her. Client, not a gal pal."

"You know where the rest of her is?"

"Nope."

"So, who the hell is the pretty lady?" Actually, at that point, not so pretty.

"Her name is...was...Valerie Garrett. As I said, she is ...was...a client. Came looking for help because she thought someone was going to murder her."

Brady whistled.

"Well, she was sure right to be worried. Hope she didn't pay you too much to keep that from happening."

Several of the street cops snorted. That Larrybrady. Funny guy.

"Look, Larry, I'll come down to Central and give you lugs a full and detailed statement. But could you just get Mrs. Garrett's head and your blue army the hell out of my damn office?"

"Sorry, Jack. You know that's not how it works. This is a crime scene. You are going to have to leave, not take anything and maybe in a couple weeks we'll release the scene."

"Aw c'mon Brady. I need my files...they're confidential for godsake...you'll put me out of business."

"Too bad Arch. Protocols are protocols."

"What do you think you're going to find in my office? A samurai sword?"

"Is that what you used?" More snorts from the blue bellies.

Brady looked at me hard.

"Before you can get too wasted on that Canadian Club, get your ass down to the station and give a full statement to Goeller. And

I mean full. Don't try pulling that privilege crap. You ain't no priest or lawyer. I'll be along later to make you do it again."

Brady nodded at a young Irish patrolman.

"Officer Cronin, haul Mr. Arch down to Central. Now. And leave the Canadian Club here. It's evidence."

I spent the next eighteen hours at police headquarters playing cop games. They took my statement. I was a good cooperative citizen. Could not have been more detailed or forthcoming. Told them all I knew. I left Thom Wheeler out of it. He added nothing to the sordid tale.

Naturally, as a reward for my fine cooperation, they threw me into a holding cell. When I asked to call my attorney, they told me I was in protective custody.

"Protection from what?"

"Protection from yourself. You're obviously a damn suicide risk."

Brady and Goeller pulled the good cop/ bad cop silliness, even flipping characters every couple hour. Finally, off stage, they apparently arrested Carson Garrett. Cops charged him with first degree murder of his wife and cut me loose with a warning to not leave town.

Larrybrady always gets his man.

I had to call a taxi from a pay phone on the street.

Chapter VI -- Carson Garrett

Carson Garrett's arrest and trial were huge news, in town and around the country. Not surprising, given the macabre particulars of Valerie Garrett's last moments, the High Society angle and Mrs. Garrett's sultry pulchritude. Mae West joked on the radio that she'd cut off her own head to get that kind of publicity.

Public opinion ran hard against Carson Garrett. He got out of jail pending trial after posting the incredible $100,000 bond set by the judge. I guess Thommy Wheeler was right about the guy not being without means.

I was a big deal for a while. I borrowed Wheeler's lake house about an hour north of town to hide from the press and, ridiculously, even tourists.

After a few weeks, the fact that poor Valerie's head ended up on my desk became a minor detail. I was just one of the many prosecution witnesses who would testify that Valerie Garrett claimed her husband intended to kill her.

Most of the other witnesses to Mrs. Garrett's claims were far above me in the societal and cultural food chains. Including, by golly, my old buddy Thom Wheeler who remembered hearing the late Mrs. Garrett predict spousalcide at the Pacific-Union Club bar a few weeks before her decapitation. That Wheeler never mentioned that to me was a curiosity. That he never invited me to the Pacific-Union Club was a damn outrage.

A few weeks before the trial, Carson Garrett walked into my office. As with his wife many eventful months before, I nodded for Garrett to sit in that same hardback wooden chair aside my desk. He had lost some weight and was tan. He looked good. Even the hair looked kinda natural.

"Good morning, Mr. Arch."

I shrugged. "Good morning Mr. Garrett."

"You're probably surprised to see me here."

Another nod from me. Shocked was more like it.

"I want to hire you to find Valerie's killer."

"Look, Garrett, I don't know what your game is. Your late wife sat there and blew smoke up my kimono. Maybe you Garretts just like yanking my chain for some perverse reason."

Garrett held up his hand to get me to stop but I continued.

"I'm sure the pricks at Whitefield, Mason and Green have an army of talented, expensive investigators turning over every stone."

Garrett smiled wanly and waved his hand dismissively.

"Of course, they do and they are. But those guys are only looking for evidence that casts enough reasonable doubt on my motives and opportunities to convince a jury."

I rubbed my face in exaggerated weariness.

"Well, in the course of their investigations, they're likely to tumble onto the real killer, assuming it's not you."

Garrett let that go.

"Nah. They take as granted that I didn't do it. That's all they want to prove. They don't care who did do it. Not their problem. The prosecution, at the end of the day, only has a bunch of people like you saying Valerie believed that I wanted her dead."

He put both hands on my desk and leaned in.

"They don't have a weapon. They don't have any physical evidence but poor Valerie's head. I was home in bed. I can't prove that I was. They can't prove that I wasn't. They have no compelling motive. I loved my wife."

I looked up. "What about the insurance?"

"Yeah, there was some insurance. Old policies. And, of course, the bastards are sitting on the payout hoping I get convicted and they skate. The cops even speculated that I was so pissed off at you after our little luncheon chat that I went home, chopped off my wife's head and sent it to you in a stationer's box."

He sat back and held his hands apart.

"Then got rid of a ton of incriminating evidence before they kicked down my door a few hours later. They got nothing."

"Why me? There are plenty of other investigators who would be glad to take your money and chase down empty leads forever."

"Why? Because, Mr. Arch, I believe you actually did care about Valerie and wanted to protect her. You pissed me off at the Princess that day but confronting me went to more than just that three hundred dollars."

Garrett leaned forward again and looked me in the eye.

"And whoever did it made a point of sending her head here. You got some connection to this mess. I think you're the only guy around who can chase Valerie's killer down."

One final shrug.

"Sorry, Garrett, no can do. I'm testifying against you in a capital murder case in a few weeks. There are all kinds of professional ethics and conflicts of interest here. And, frankly, I'm sick of the Garrett clan."

Carson Garrett stood up, pursed his thin lips, and stuck out his soft, manicured right hand. "Okay," he said, "got it."

I looked up at Garrett.

"Good luck. I'm sorry for your loss and, for the record, I don't believe you killed Valerie. Have your attorney ask me that at the trial. I'll get it out before the prosecution can object. The judge will toss my opinion, but it'll be in the jurors' heads. You only need one of them to agree with me."

Carson Garrett nodded his chin and left my office. I never saw him again, outside of the courtroom.

Chapter VII -- The Lake House

The pricks from Whitefield, Mason and Green and their investigators did a good job. After a sensational, six-week trial and four days of deliberations, Carson Garrett was found not guilty by a jury of his peers.

The legitimate press and the scandal sheets did not agree with the verdict. But they quickly moved on to the next big ink eater involving a City Alderman and a carnally precocious schoolgirl.

I like to think that the Garrett jury was influenced to some degree by the inappropriate blurting of my opinion of our boy's innocence in open court. The folks who license Private Investigators in California took a dim view of my shenanigans but only issued a strongly worded letter of disapproval. I kept my license.

In the late Fall, I bummed Thom Wheeler's lake house for a few days. The cabin is on a secluded lake tucked into the wine country. It is beautifully decorated in teak and authentic Japanese antiques and appointments.

The cabin is a great hideout. I sometimes am lucky and bring a lady along. This time I was flying solo.

I poured three fingers of Canadian Club and strolled down by the lake. The air was crisp. I sipped the CC and watched the sun dropping below the tree line.

As I turned to hustle back to the cabin, a shadow on the edge of the woods caught my eye. Something looked irregular. I approached and stared at a slight door-shaped depression in the soft soil next to the woods.

"I hope Ol' Thommy didn't plant a little garden over here this Summer. That would not do at all."

As the sun settled further, the illusion of a door-shaped depression disappeared, and the ground again looked natural and undisturbed.

Just as I had left it all those months ago.

Sipping my highball, I spoke to the evening.

"Well, Valerie, my little Veronica Lake. You got a great spot here close to a lake almost as beautiful as you. Maybe we should call it Valerie Lake. Your lovely blonde head rests peacefully in a crypt at Mission Dolores. This is much nicer. Enjoy the Winter, darling."

As I walked away, I toasted Valerie's four charming neighbors there in the loam by the woods.

"You ladies enjoy the chilly days too. I'll see you next Spring. I miss you all dearly."

Returning to the cabin, I felt the first stirring of the hunger returning. I smiled in anticipation. I finished my drink, climbed into the big cannonball bed, and fell asleep immediately.

In the Still of the Night

Notable Author: Eileen McIntire (Nov 2020)

Genre: Cozy Mystery
Prompt: Using no more than 100 words, pick an elderly character, describe their setting, and create the crime they are to solve.

Prompt Forward

Abe Cronin was a legend on Johnson Heights. Lived in the house of his birth, war hero, retired success, and consummate busy-body. He was the busiest busy-body in a small city of overachieving busy-bodies.

The night the still exploded on Hilltop Drive, Abe was playing Red-dog poker with some dodgy acquaintances in the backroom of Brown's. The blast, two blocks away, knocked Abe, as he said, "onto my double-negative."

Spry in spite of his years, Abe hurried to investigate the smoky red flame. From the tumult, a skinny teenager barreled into Abe almost knocking him again onto his double-negative.

"Honest to Pete, Mister Cronin, I'd nothing to do with it. Hope Addie's okay."

With that, the kid was gone.

Chapter 1: Hilltop and Louisiana

A gaggle of neighborhood usuals had already caucused at the corner of Hilltop Drive and Louisiana Avenue watching the conflagration. Abe joined the gapers.

"Damn, Lyons is going to be pissed when he sees what those Welsh morons done to his house." Walt Davis sucked on his Camel.

An anonymous questioner from the rear snorted.

"What the hell did Lyons have those idiots making shine in his house for anyway? For crap's sake, he's General Manager at the paper. He's got a job. A damn good job. He didn't need the extra."

Davis again, "Well, I'll tell ya, those Welsh brothers made some good hooch."

A woman's voice. "They were cousins."

Still another contributor to the proceedings offered a clarification.

"Hell, they're from down around Romney. Those in-bred West Virginia Mountain boys don't know whether they're brothers or cousins or both."

Laughter all around

Abe finally spoke. And when Abe spoke, the assembled listened.

"Those Welsh fellas are probably in the middle of that hell fire cooking like steak, Pittsburgh style. We might want to show a little respect. I don't see Lyon's car so, hopefully, he's not home. But doesn't he have a child?"

Before anyone answered, a wailing fire engine...Braddock Fire Department's proud hook and ladder...came haul-assing up Louisiana and spun onto Hilltop. The firefighting professionals had no trouble finding the house ablaze.

Phil Smith whistled. "Damn the city foundation savers got here before the volunteer guys. I'd have lost that bet."

"It's bingo night. That always slows them volunteer boys down."

The first responders quickly and astutely realized that the house on fire was a goner. Kaput. So they set about trying to make sure the entire neighborhood didn't also get consumed. Their past record in that regard was not good.

Fortunately, the Lyons' house sat between an alley and a vacant lot, and the contiguous homes outside those barriers were both sturdy brick affairs. The BFD hosed those babies so that no embers could set them ablaze.

The residents of those unfortunate homes had escaped unharmed and were desperately alerting the fire professionals that most of the windows in their homes had been blown out by the explosion. The water pouring from the recently arrived pump truck was not really very helpful.

Several cruisers from the Braddock Police Department arrived on site and stern-faced officers were insistently ordering folks who were standing well back from the blaze to "stand back." They were stern and insistent.

A clanking, rattling 1929 DeSoto Six was next to come flying up Louisiana.

"Well, there's Lyons," shrugged Phil Smith, "I guess he ain't getting parboiled. Good thing he works on the morning paper. Probably downtown when his house blew up."

The coupe's croup was lost in the cacophony of the roaring blaze, and the many civil servants attending to their official duties.

Phil Smith, never satisfied, joined the noise.

"Why doesn't he get that car fixed? It's only two years old. Company car, for chrissakes. Old man Fitzpatrick should take it away from Lyons if he's too lazy or dumb to take care of it. A damn fine car."

Gary Lyons, recently a homeowner and still Managing Director of the Braddock Morning-Herald Newspaper, shut off and jumped out of his laboring DeSoto. He frantically ran from fireman to cop, screaming questions. They all shook their heads negatively and got back to their jobs.

A distraught Lyons ran over to the assembled voyeurs at Hilltop and Louisiana. He spotted Abe.

"Abe, I couldn't remember where I parked, has anyone seen my Adele? Is she here? For god's sake, tell me she's around here somewhere. She was supposed to be here."

Abe didn't know Adele.

"Gary, I'm sure she's okay. She'll turn up. We'll all be praying for her. And you."

Gary Lyons sat on the curb at Hilltop and Louisiana and bawled. The gaggle of curious had gone silent and his sobs were lost to the roaring blaze and the officious shouting of uniformed municipal employees.

Chapter 2: Billy Faraccio

Next morning, Abe was atop his normal perch in the backroom at Brown's. The only other alter cocker there then was Pat Lafferty, a retired cop.

"Pat, you know that skinny kid used to deliver papers all over the Heights?"

Lafferty appreciated that Abe called him Pat, not Paddy like all the a-holes on the Johnson Heights. Just because he once drove the wagon. Man.

"Yeah, Abe, I know who you mean. Tall, pin ass kid, right? The hell's his name?"

Abe gave Pat a moment. He'd get there. Once a cop, always a cop.

"Billy...Billy Faraccio. That's it. He was the paperboy for everyone up here. Lives down in Barbara Fritchie Village with his folks. Boatload of Faraccios down there."

"He still delivering for the Herald?"

"Don't think so. I've been getting mine from some older guy, used to work at the tire plant till he got furloughed. Think Billy is gone. Why?"

"Nothing. Thought I saw him last night in all the hubbub. Just curious."

"Ain't no one more curious than you, Cronin."

Abe finished his coffee and said goodbye to the gang who had grown from just Pat to seven pissers.

"See you turd blossoms tomorrow."

The Maryland Avenue streetcar stopped outside Brown's. Abe hopped on and rode it all the way down to Barbara Fritchie Village, south of the underpass. The area was okay for pilgrims during daylight. After dark, you'd better be a local and it wouldn't hurt to be carrying a tire thumper.

Abe asked around. Wasn't hard to get a bead on the Faraccios. They lived on the end of a block of slap dash row houses. They had nine kids in a house too small for a family of four. That was not uncommon in South Braddock and Abe wondered, not for the first time, how so many brats could be conceived in such a raucous environment. He and Betty couldn't make one baby in forty years of sad privacy.

Abe anticipated a busy time trying to locate Billy among this family dynamic. Nope, first thing Abe sees after turning onto the block is Billy strolling Abe's way, his demeanor much less frantic than last evening.

Billy saw Abe and grinned.

"Hey, Mr. Cronin. What're you doing down here in the Village?"

"Looking for you, young man." Abe smiled.

"Me? Really? Well, here I am."

Abe looked at the kid. Skinny as a popsicle stick. Tumbleweed head of black hair. Next whisker would be his first. Probably be a handsome young man in a few years.

"Billy, my boy, you remember the last time we ran into each other?"

"I don't know. Guess, back when I still worked for the paper?"

"Actually, Billy, it was last night. And ran into each other is what we did. You practically knocked me over barrel-assing away from the Lyons house that'd just exploded. Remember?"

Billy looked down at his scruffy shoes.

"No, sir, that wasn't me. I was nowhere near there last night. I was down at the old basin all night. Just came home to say 'hey' to my folks. Don't like worrying 'em too much."

"Billy," Abe asked with a cocked eyebrow, "now what do you know about me?"

Billy lit up. "I heard you killed 150 Hun during the Great War. More than Sergeant York. That right?"

"Well, Billy, let's say that is right. Do you think I could kill 150 Germans with poor eyesight?"

"Probably not."

"No sir, Billy. I could not. I got very good eyesight. I know what I saw last evening. I know who ran into me. It was Billy Faraccio. Who now stands before me talking fibs to his shoes, rather than truth to this old coot."

Billy scuffed his right shoe in the dirt of Barbara Fritchie Village.

"Sorry, Mr. Cronin, I just…I just a…"

"Billie, you mentioned Addie when you bounced off me. Hoped she was okay. Billy, do you know where Adele Lyons is? Her old man's worried to death about her."

"That bastard? Piss on him."

"Where's Adele, Billy?"

Billy looked at Abe Cronin.

"If I tell you, Mr. Cronin, you gotta promise not to tell no one else."

Abe Cronin tried to make his scowl look like something that would soil the pants of 150 German infantrymen.

"Where's Adele, young man? Now!"

"She's down at our place in the basin. One of the boats."

"Your place? What the hell? You live in one of those rotting canal boats? For godssake. Let's go, Billy."

Chapter 3: The Canal Basin

The old canal, never very prosperous after railroads came along, was finally washed away, and bankrupted by the Flood of '26. Braddock had been its western terminus, the canal stopped by soaring mountains that defied canal engineers then and forever.

A parcel of downtown Braddock was given over to a large basin, watered by the river and chock-a-block with low, flat canal boats. Mules pulled those boats back and forth to Richmond. Surrounding the basin had been boat building operations, warehouses, coal piles, saloons, and brothels. All gone now. Mostly.

The basin, cut off from the river's refills, had mostly evaporated away in the five years since the floods. Dozens of abandoned canal boats lay aground on the basin's bottom. All the boats were rotting derelicts, made of cheap-ass lumber, and biodegrading like snowballs in a soup pot. Hobos and destitute folks clinging to the lowest ladder of society made homes in some of these boats, if they couldn't find a nicer abode under a train trestle.

Abe and Billy Faraccio stepped carefully into one of these palaces. The original living quarters was a small wooden block with two windows that sat on the boat's deck. Additional room was now theoretically available in the rotting cargo hold. Billy and Adele had wisely chosen to leave that space to the rat-eating snakes and the snake-eating rats who were homesteading there.

Adele was a comely fifteen-year-old. Her fetchingness no doubt due in some part to the better than modest financial circumstances of Gary Lyons, her father. She was also clearly pregnant.

"Hello, Adele. Can I call you Addie?"

"Sure, Mr. Cronin."

"You know me?"

"Everybody knows you, Mr. Cronin."

"Hmm. I see. So one of you tell me what the hell is going on?"

Billy began.

"Well, as you know, I used to deliver newspapers for the Herald. I had the biggest route of any deliverer in Braddock, except for the guys who worked the hospitals and the westside rich folks."

Billy smiled at Adele.

"I had over 250 customers. They all loved me. I gave them good service. I was making more money, a lot more money, than my old man at the synthetic silk plant. And he has nine kids to feed, for godssake."

Abe nodded, "Go on."

"Anyway, my customers loved me. And Mr. Lyons loved me. I was his boy. Till me and Addie started up. He didn't know at first. We kept it a secret. We would sneak down here and…you know…"

Addie chimed in "…do boy and girl stuff."

Abe rubbed his brow and shook his head. "Continue."

"Yeah, so, boy and girl stuff. Then Addie started missin and we kinda figured she was going to have a baby. No problem for me. I love Addie. Like I said I was making man money. I'd saved some.

I used to lose a lot playing pinball at Shaw's but I promised Addie I'd stop. And I did. And I quit school. I was a man now. School is for kids and fools."

"Oh, hell, "Abe sighed.

"Anyway, "Adele takes over, "I started to get a belly and bigger up top so we decided to tell my Daddy about us. How we were going to get married and all. Have his grandchild."

"Let me guess. Your Daddy didn't take the news too well."

Billy snorted.

"Oh, hell no, he punched me in the jaw…not much of a punch really, I've been hit worse in the alley…and fired me on the spot. He threw me out of their house. Then he threw Adele out on the street too."

Adele, red-eyed, hissed.

"That bastard has been making moonshine in the cellar for years with those Welsh goons. Where does he get being so high and mighty. Threw his own kin and grandkin right out onto Hilltop Drive."

Billy hugged Adele.

"We don't care. We've been making it so far. I'll find a job somehow. I know it's tough since the crash. We're in love and we're going to make this work."

Abe looked at the girl.

"Adele, you need to tell your father you're not a pile of ashes in that house like those Welsh boys. He's worried out of his mind. If you don't tell him, I will."

"If you do, Mr. Cronin, I swear Billy and I will jump on the next freight train to Cincinnati and no one in Braddock will ever see us or this baby ever again. I swear."

Abe Cronin looked at the couple, this hillbilly Romeo and Juliet.

"Okay, I won't tell for now. But you two come stay at my house till we get this sorted out. There's plenty of room. I'm up on Johnson Heights. You'll have to be careful sneaking in and out. You seem pretty good at that. I won't even care about the boy and girl stuff."

Adele blushed and said, "That's kind of you Mr. Cronin but we'll stay here for now. We just need to find Billy a new job."

Exhausted, Abe sat on a hard wooden bench.

"You two… Okay, Billy, I want you to meet me at the N&W roundhouse tomorrow at 7:30 sharp. General Superintendent's office. Got it?"

"Yessir. But, Mr. Cronin, there's one other thing."

"Go on, Billy."

"Last night, I decided to go face Mr. Lyons, try to get my deliverer job back. I was coming up that alley that runs up from Sherman Place to Hilltop Drive next to Addie's house…old house. And I heard Mr. Lyons turn off Sherman Pace and start up the alley too."

"Keep going Billy."

"Well, I chickened out and ducked behind some bushes. Mr. Lyons parked his car halfway down the alley. I know it's his car because it makes so much racket and I guess he didn't want anyone hearing him. Anyway, Mr. Lyons sneaks up to his house and I see him with a big jar with a rag sticking out the top. He lights the rag with his lighter then throws the bottle into an open cellar window."

Billy squeezed Adele tighter.

"He walks back to his car…don't know why he wasn't running…gets in his car, backs down the alley and takes off. A few minutes later…kaboom. I'm thinking if folks see me, they're going to think I did it. So I ran like hell and that's when I crashed into you."

"You positive it was Lyons?"

"It was definitely his car but I didn't see his face."

Adele looks at Abe.

"He thought I was coming home last night. I'd sent a note to his office saying I was, to have it out with him. He was trying to kill me. And the baby. Sure glad I chickened out too."

Abe rubbed his chin thinking "I have got to get out of this busybody business."

Then he turns to Billy, "7:30 sharp."

"Yes, sir, Mr. Cronin."

"One last question Addie, does your father smoke?"

"No sir, never has."

"I'll see you kids later."

Chapter 4: Vincent D. Fitzpatrick III

The next morning, Billy Feraccio sat outside the General Superintendent's office at the N&W roundhouse waiting for Abe Cronin. The door opens and out stepped Abe and another man, impressively dressed and ramrod straight.

"Billy, this is General Superintendent Doogan."

Billy looked like the scruffy street kid he was, but he stuck out his hand and said, "Mr. Doogan."

Mr. Doogan chuckled, shook Billy's hand, and said, "Pleasure meeting you son."

Abe put his hand on Billy's shoulder.

"At my recommendation, Mr. Doogan has agreed to take you on as a stringer here at the yards. That means, you'll do whatever task he or any supervisor tells you to do. You'll get here every day by 7:00 am, even weekends, and work till there's no more work for you to do that day. Got it?"

"Yes, sir."

"Now Billy you will not be getting paid. You'll be learning lots of jobs around the office and shops. Eventually, some position will open up and if Mr. Doogan thinks you're worthy and ready, you'll be put on a seniority roster and you'll start getting paid."

"Yes, sir. I Understand."

"Don't let me down Billy. Remember all those Hun. You don't want me mad at you."

"Yes sir. I will not let anyone down."

Abe fished a $5 bill out of his pocket and gave it to Billy.

"The stores downtown are open late tonight. Go down to the Manhattan and buy some cheap but sturdy work clothes, including underwear. Wash those clothes at least once a week at your folks' house or come over to my place. Come to work clean. Respect your job. Got it."

Abe turned to Doogan and said, "Thanks Carl. Keep me apprised."

"I will John. Great seeing you again."

Abe took the Virginia Avenue streetcar downtown then walked over to the basin to check on Adele. As he approached the canal boat, a tall, well-dressed fellow emerged from the cabin door. Abe ducked behind a pile of rotting skiffs.

The well-dressed man tucked his head furtively into his hat and scuttled away, towards the business district.

Abe shook his head, "What the hell?" Abe Cronin knocked on the cabin door.

"Forget something?" Adele opened the door. "Oh, hi Mr. Cronin."

"Hello Adele, may I come in?"

Adele stepped aside and Abe entered.

"Adele...Addie...I was stopping by to try once more to get you to let your father know you're okay. He's still sick over your disappearance. But then I see young Vincent Fitzpatrick leaving here and now I have other questions."

"He's just a friend, Mr. Cronin. Honest. He just brought me a present."

"What kind of present?"

Adele took a $20 bill from her pocket.

"That's quite a present. Is it your birthday?"

"No. Mr. Fitzpatrick just likes giving me presents once in a while."

Abe Cronin stared at Adele and could see her defenses melting.

"Adele, is Mr. Fitzpatrick your baby's father?"

Adele rocked back. "No way. Billy is the baby's father. Just Billy."

"Um hmm. Well, is it just remotely possible, just crazy possible, that Fitzpatrick is the daddy?"

Adele's eyes welled up. "Yes. It is possible."

"And how long has that boy girl stuff been going on?"

"It's over. We stopped…stuff…when Vince found out I was knocked up."

Vince.

"Now, he just stops by every week or so and gives me some money. Cause he's worried about me…and the baby."

"Does Billy know?"

"No, he just thinks I have some money from when I lived at home. It's how we live since Billy got fired."

"Oh, Adele, you are one complicated little girl."

"Don't I know it."

Abe gave her a hug and took his leave. And walked straight to the downtown Hibernia Club. Abe was a big damn deal at the Hibernia Club, though he seldom went there. His life's accomplishments made every Irish- American in town, from the top of the social ladder to the bottom, proud. He never paid dues at the Club, or paid a tab. Someone always took care of them, and folks fought for the honor.

Vincent D. Fitzpatrick III was lunching at the bar as he did every day and as Abe knew he did every day. Abe stepped beside him.

"Okay if I join you, Vince?"

"My god, Abe, yes. Sit down. This is an honor."

"So, Vince, how is everything going? Work? Home?"

"Oh, Abe, you know. You've been there. Dad wants me to leave the paper and go into politics. He's going to have the Herald endorse Roosevelt because he's certain Roosevelt is going to win and, when he does, he'll toss me a judgeship or something to get my political career going."

"Has the paper ever endorsed a Democrat?"

"Never."

Abe chuckled and shook his head.

"Dad paid for my law school and he isn't going to be satisfied until I'm Governor or a Senator."

"Is that bad?"

"Abe, you're about the most life experienced man I know. I'm not a bad man. But I have done things I'm not proud of. In the war, in school, in my marriage. I'm trying to change. Be a good man. Maybe not as good a man as you. But good enough for myself."

"I see," said Abe.

"I know that if I go into politics, I will be corrupted beyond redemption. I will grow to really hate myself. And those around me, who I love, will grow to hate me too."

"What does your wife say?"

"Oh, she's ambivalent. Ever since we found out we couldn't have kids…no V.D.F. the Fourth…she's been depressed. I don't think being a Senator's wife is going to change anything."

"What's your dad say?"

"Hell. He doesn't want to hear any of that crap. Full speed ahead on the Senator thing. If we weren't Irish and Catholic, he'd want me to divorce Edith and marry someone who can have the 'Fourth.' He's not someone who is particularly troubled by conscience. You know him as well as anyone."

"Vince, I am not the paragon you think I am. Most people in town think I won that Medal of Honor at Belleau Wood. You were at Belleau Wood too, so you probably know this story."

Abe sipped his iced tea.

"I received that damn Medal of Honor for the Philippines in 1902. I led some Marines in Luzon against a nest of Filipino freedom fighters. They fought like bastards but we finally killed them all and I got the big medal. You with me?"

"Sure, Abe, fascinating. Go on."

"What I most remember of that day, as we're marching away, all the women screaming at us, calling us every name in the book, because we slaughtered their husbands, fathers, and brothers. Those guys, those warriors who fought like bastards, were defending their homes from invaders. Us. We were the real bastards. And I was the biggest bastard of all, and I have a medal to prove it."

"I think you're being too hard on yourself, Abe. Hells bells, man, you were just following orders. Doing what your country asked you to do."

"Doing what my country inappropriately asked me to do. Right after that Luzon battle, I mustered out and came home and joined the railroad and started trying to purge my guilt. Like you, Betty and I couldn't have kids so I did what I could to help other people's kids. "

"You're rightfully famous for that."

"Well, when we finally jumped in in 1917, I went down to re-enlist. Betty and all my friends thought me nuts. They were sure the Marines wouldn't take me back. But they sure as hell did. Best thing that Medal of Honor ever did for me."

Abe looked at Fitzpatrick and shook his head.

"They made me a major and sent me right to the front. As you know, it was hairy as hell at Belleau Wood. But I was finally on the side of righteousness. I only got a DSC that time, but that's the medal I wear in the parades. That was my redemption."

"Damn, Abe. That is about the best lesson I have ever received. Thank you."

"Go make your wife and yourself proud. That might mean telling Vincent, Jr to pound sand. Think you can do that?"

"That's a good question Abe. A good question."

Chapter 5: Vincent D. Fitzpatrick Jr

Abe Cronin stood in the mahogany corporate office of the Braddock Morning-Herald. He noticed Gary Lyons' office was dark. Probably taking some time off to deal with the tumult in his life.

"Mr. Cronin, nice to see you again, how can I help you."

"Laura, I'd like a few minutes with Vinnie if he can fit me in."

The office manager giggled. "No one calls Mr. Fitzpatrick 'Vinnie' but you. Let me check."

A few minutes later, Laura returned and said, "He'd love to see you. Go right in."

Vincent D. Fitzpatrick, Jr. was standing. He was a tall, gaunt man, impeccably dressed.

Fitzpatrick was a few years older than Abe, but they had been amicably flying around each other's orbits since grade school at St. Pat's.

"Damn, Abe, it's great to see you. Been far too long."

"Vincent. You're looking as fearsome as ever."

Fitzpatrick laughed and waved Abe into a chair at the front of his desk. The chair was three inches lower than Fitzpatrick's chair.

"Can I get you something, Abe?"

"Do you mind if I smoke?"

"Hell, no, go ahead. Give me one too."

Abe handed the pack of Chesterfields over the desk and asked, "You gotta light?"

"You bet."

Fitzpatrick reached into his pocket and pulled out a lighter and lit each of their cigarettes.

Abe Cronin nodded to himself.

"So, Abe, what brings you down here?"

"I know what you did, Vincent. I can't prove it. But I know you did it."

"What the hell are you talking about?"

"I know you murdered those two, poor bastards from Romney who worked Gary Lyons' cellar still. You didn't mean to. You were hoping to kill Lyons' daughter Adele."

"You're crazy, Abe."

"You'll get a lot of agreement on that. You discovered your son was having an affair with a fifteen-year-old girl...the daughter of one of your employees...and that she is now pregnant."

Abe glared at the senior Fitzpatrick.

"Statutory rape and illegitimate babies are not very helpful in starting a political career. Kill the girl and the inconveniences go away."

"It might be time for you to leave Cronin."

"I must say, using Lyons' own car was genius. Company car. I'm sure you have a key. If anyone spotted you that night…which they did by-the-way…they'd think it was Lyons burning down his own damn house for some reason. Just because he's too dumb or lazy to get his timing chain adjusted."

"Dumb and lazy," snorted Fitzpatrick, "with a slut daughter."

"You're a long shot for Boss-of-the-Year, Vinnie. Anyway, everything I know is in writing and will be opened by the authorities, your son, and the Evening Standard if anything untoward happens to me, Adele, her baby, or your daughter-in-law."

That Evening Standard jab stung Fitzpatrick the most. Abe smirked.

"Won't your crosstown rivals have fun with that headline. 'Beloved Medal of Honor Recipient Names Vincent D. Fitzpatrick Jr. as His Murderer'"

Abe stood.

"Don't bother getting up Vinnie, you prick. I know the way out."

The Ozmond Conumdrum

Notable Author: Jack Campbell, i.e. John Henry (Dec, 2020)

Genre: Science Fiction
Prompt: Using just 100 words, write an intro to a sci-fi story with a flight instructor living on a future planet at harvest time and incorporate a holographic reality, an overpopulated city, and an alien attack in your piece.

Prompt Forward

The final cadet saluted and fled. Valentine cursed. He had maybe two cadets with the necessaries for Corvair training. He needed fifty.

A hologram of Marcy pinged into his office. Whatever pittance she was wearing sure wasn't straining the holo's power chamber.

"Hey, flyboy, come home and practice complex docking maneuvers with me."

Valentine whistled.

"Can't do it. Got Ozmonds marauding on both moons, rail-gunning the force shields protecting Tartzian pickers and 38-million bedwetters in New Baltimore praying we save the crops and them."

Marcy, now completely starkers, sighed.

"Okay, hero, if you prefer beets to me, I'll bubble-bath alone."

Chapter One: New Baltimore, Planet of Tartz

The Tartzians were not picking beets. They were picking floco, a delicate poppy-like flower that only grew, as far as the experts could determine, on the planet of Tartz, an earthlike orb with two moons. Tartz was identified as colonizable several hundred Earth years before by an advanced Voyager probe. It possessed an agreeable oxygen rich atmosphere, plenty of water and a 1.2 g gravitational tug.

Soon after Tartz's discovery, two-hundred massive Mayflower colonizing arks made the arduous, twelve blackhole tunnel jump journey from Earth at .999 warp speed. All the arks miraculously survived with their one million pod cargo of colonists, and accompanying organic specimens, technological do-dads and pre-fab housing and machinery required to boost the colony- success analytics to an acceptable forecast.

The Tartz colony, unlike many other woe-begotten human colonies, was a rip-roaring success. Thanks to the impressive fecundity of the original colonists and their issue, and the constant influx of new immigrants, almost three hundred million humans inhabited and prospered on Tartz.

The capital city of the Tartz Territory was New Baltimore, named after a long-ago flooded city on Earth Prime (and, apparently, some long forgotten big sneeze from the also long-ago flooded Britannia islets). New Baltimore was built upon the delta and feeding valleys of the Whoseafrades and Tigger Rivers, which flowed into the Hawking Sea. Its fine harbor and fortunate location made for a natural center of governance and economic prominence.

While the territorial ruling nabobs might have disagreed, the overarching driver for New Baltimore's prominence and location was the floco. The wispy plant grew wild as a localized species. The first Earth colonists tried harvesting floco to determine if it had any dietary or pharmaceutical qualities. While native fauna coexisted with floco, whenever any alien or alien's machinery merely touched the floco, it would collapse immediately into a microscopic powder that also resisted any kind of analysis. Floco is the shortened form of floccinaucinihilipilification, an old word meaning "worthless."

Tartz had a large and varied fauna and flora. Many of the animals and plants were found to be useful for human consumption, and other adaptations. None of the plants or animals had evolved to high cognitive or self-aware states, although several human organizations lobbied aggressively on their behalf with the nabobs. To little effect.

Curiously, after seven generations of human colonization near New Baltimore, descendants of early settlers were found to have developed a dermatological enzyme that allowed them to touch the floco without causing it to self-vaporize. Machines could still not touch the floco in the field but machinery treated with excretions from "floco-sensitive" could handle the flower and its extractions in lab settings. The plant had to be hand harvested by Mayflower descendants, an arduous and humbling labor.

Some fifty years before Jack Valentine faced defending New Baltimore from Ozmond war chiefs, scientists at a MIT facility on one of Tartz's moons…Beyoncé…made the incredible discovery that floco had properties that could facilitate time travel. They'd mixed floco extract into the fuel of their crude time machines and damn if the machines didn't just up and disappear, presumably to some other time.

While its basic chemical composition was straightforward, floco defied synthetization or transplantation. Only floco from the New Baltimore delta region possessed the enigmatic properties that scientists were convinced would lead to unlocking the mysteries of the time space continuum.

Overnight, the floco crop became perhaps the top strategic commodity in the known universes. As New Baltimore's growth exploded, the High Consortium directed the construction of the most impregnable force shield ever built over the entire New Baltimore delta area, including the floco fields. Defensive airbases were positioned within the perimeter of the force shield protected area, with deep tunnels connecting to the outlying training and forward deployed attack positions. Colonel Jack Valentine commanded these units. They were the only air combat assets on Tartz.

The High Consortium included most of the technologically advanced civilizations. Known rogue civilizations were technologically immature. In time, leadership considered the defensive measures around New Baltimore to be overdone, classic belts and suspenders. That both the flower and potential harvesters were exclusive to the New Baltimore region only reinforced the thinking that the floco crop was safe. The MIT Lab moved back to New Baltimore and the air units were quietly transitioned to training facilities for young pilots. Slow progress was made on the time travel project. The temporal engineers and scientists on the project never lost faith in believing the inherent qualities of the floco were essential to success.

New Baltimore was a bustling metropolis with an economy built around the government, sea trade and floco. Floco harvests and siloed stores were very carefully monitored. Theft for illegal resale occurred infrequently and, practically, was fraught given the very fragile nature of the crop and the high tech needed to store and transport it.

The almost forty million human residents of New Baltimore lived very nice safe lives until the Ozmonds appeared in high orbit, invading the moons, and firing atomic rail guns at the force shield. These stalwart pampered citizens quickly became, as Jack Valentine observed, bedwetters.

Chapter Two: Jack Meets Gloria

Colonel Valentine commanded his office, literally his office, to summon Captain Mitchell.

Instantly, his office door opened and in marched Captain Peggy "Hap" Mitchell, Valentine's chief aide. She was, in Valentine's opinion, the most miserable, dyspeptic, sorry-ass person he had ever met. Naturally, she was a brilliant and formidable aide and nick-named "Hap." She hated the nickname.

"Sir."

"Where do we stand, Peggy, on the S. O. S.?"

"As you know from yesterday's conversation, our request for assistance was sent as a high priority to HCHQ almost ten days ago. Assuming the black holes and dark matter are not misbehaving, our message will not be received for about another five days."

Hap paused for effect. Valentine gave a silent hurry-up.

"Their response or HQ based deployment of help would take another 15 days to get back here. Even if they have assets between here and HQ, by the time those assets received new orders and came here, it's still going to vector out to about 15 days. Best scenario, we could hear from HCHQ in 20 days. Yesterday, I estimated 21 days."

Valentine looked at Mitchell in high sardonic.

"Thanks, Peggy, for the update. Everything still the same with the shield? She holding okay?"

"Dr. Cardamone, in his morning briefing to the governor and us, said the shield was holding. Seemed fine. The Ozmonds had upgraded to hyper-sonic, atomic munitions which came as a surprise."

Another dramatic pause. Another hurry-up hand wave.

"The literature on the Ozmonds is that they're rogue brigands, pirates who terrorize and plunder under-defended communities. They were not thought to have this level of sophisticated weaponry."

"What do our scans show? Save me the sarcasm of having asked you this before."

"The mothership appears to have four forward facing railguns. It has deployed combat units and tactical nukes to each of the moons, Beyoncé, and Turtle. We successfully evacuated both moons of their small garrisons when the Ozmonds first popped through. You probably know that since you lead the evacs."

"Anything new, Mitchell?"

"We are seeing many more space fighters buzzing around the mothership. There is still no force shield around the mothership. If we had a railgun or two of our own, we could blow that thing back to wherever Ozmond central is."

"How do their space fighters appear?"

"They're not Corvairs, but they seem to be quick and agile and their piloting looks competent. Maybe, they're just showing off for us, putting their best flyers out there. But if you're thinking of going after that ship before the calvary arrives, as I know the hell you are, I think we're going to be in for some even-steven dogfighting. We have better ships but rookie pilots. Isn't your dictum that it's not the ships that win, it's the pilots?"

"Of course, Mitchell, every flight commander since whenever has said that. It's like a good little guy can beat a bad big guy. It's BS. You don't know until you're in the middle of a fracas what's actually going to determine the winner."

Valentine's monitor pinged and again Marcy appeared in a hologram still starkers.

"Hey war hero, wanna come home now. I'm having a special medal presentation?"

"Beat it, Marcy. I'm here with Captain Mitchell."

"Oops. Pardonez-moi. Hi Peggy, glad we're all girls here. See you later Jack. We can talk more about me beating it."

The hologram popped off.

The Colonel looked at Mitchell's disapproving face.

"Sorry. I don't know how she does that. That hologram is supposed to be bulletproof, but she pops in whenever she wants to needle me. Her brother's a crazy-smart techie over at MIT Labs. I think he juiced up her broadcaster somehow."

"Anything else, sir?"

"Yes. I want you to check with our tech guys and get some estimate of how much computing power, memory etc., a robot would need to absorb the entire combat flight manual of a Corvair, including every nano-second of actual combat and combat simulation data we have. I don't care about the basic flying protocols, just the bang-bang stuff."

"Got it. You're nuts but I'll get on that pronto."

"Excellent, Peggy. And one last thing, I want to meet the CTOs of any and all humanoid robotics manufacturers that are here in New Baltimore. That needs to be pronto too."

"Yes sir."

"Thank you, Captain."

Jack went home that evening to their place in Bolton Hill. Marcy did her best to help the Colonel decompress from his fraught duties. Later, they played chess.

The next morning Valentine asked Captain Mitchell for an update.

"Still no word from HCHQ. I estimate approximately 19 days before we hear back from them."

Mitchell could not have been more deadpan.

"Feel better, Captain? Go on."

"Dr. Cardemone reported this morning that the force shield was still holding against the Ozmond barrage. He definitely seemed antsy while trying to project great confidence The pols were clearly unnerved by his report."

"That is worrisome."

"I spoke to our techies and they estimate the storage requirement for the Corvair combat capabilities manual, as well as all the actual, theoretical and simulation combat data and analytics would require three to four terabytes."

"My lord, that much?"

"Yep."

Valentine rubbed his face in frustration. "Anything else?"

"Yes, sir. There are three fully self-contained, humanoid robotics manufacturers in New Baltimore. They make robots for a variety of domestic and commercial applications."

Mitchell smirked. "You still wanna chat with their CTOs?"

"Yes, I do."

"Well, they'll all be here at 1400. Do you want to meet with them singularly or as a group,"

"As a group. They're each other's competitors. Sometimes that group dynamic can be useful."

"I'll take care of it, Colonel."

At 1400 hours, Peggy marched three folks into Valentine's office. Two were fortyish, baldish, types bedecked in the lightweight business outfits worn by techies since Bill Gates. The third CTO was a woman of indeterminate age dressed in a black pencil skirt, and purple long sleeve tee. She was slender, blonde, and striking. And she knew it.

Peggy asked, "Colonel, you want me to make the intros?"

"I can take it from here, Peggy, thank you."

"Sir," Peggy withdrew with a nod.

Valentine cleared his throat, "Okay, folks, I don't want to waste anymore of your time than is necessary, I just…"

"Mind if I smoke?"

All three men turned to gaze at the woman.

Before Valentine answered to forbid her lighting, one of the men barked.

"I certainly do mind your smoking, Gloria. I have asthma and it's a disgusting habit and I'm sure you're still smoking those little stinky cigars."

The blonde cocked an appraising eyebrow at Valentine who nodded.

"What he said. Ix-nay on the oking-smay."

Gloria smiled a half-amused, half-sneer smile, but said nothing more.

"Okay, as I was saying, "Valentine continued, "I'll make this quick. The government would like to purchase four or five dozen of your humanoid robots for a special military project. We need robots with very advanced, large, and small motor skills, as much internal memory capacity as you can provide, and all within a humanoid platform of a standard military pilot, say five-eight to six-one, one-hundred fifty to one-hundred-ninety pounds."

Valentine pointed to the first man.

"Okay, asthma man, tell me who you are, what your company does, and react to my requirements."

"I am Mike Wolf. My firm is First Care. We manufacture the finest caregiver bots on Tartz. They are capable of highly advanced medical and personal care assistance along the full spectrum of possible patient needs. We make several humanoid models, that bring not only high skills to their duties, but also project great empathy, humor, and patience. Their height and weight are within your specs."

Valentine nodded, "And memory capacity?"

"Fully tricked out, within the humanoid platform, the max cap is 800 gigs, with 500 or so needed to power the basic motor skills, the rest given over to customized applications."

"So you only can allocate 300 gig or so to specialized applications? And, secondly, how many bots are in your current inventory here in New Baltimore?"

"Yes, 300 gigs is about right, and we are an industry leader in this regard. Our bots offer the latest in AI capabilities which allow them to bring the absolute best care to our customers."

Gloria snorted. Valentine shot her a look.

"Continue, Mr. Wolfe. Inventory?"

"We have 30 or so bots ready for end-user customization in the warehouse. We could probably up our out-put to ten to twelve units a week if the demand was there."

Valentine made some quick notes.

"Thank you, Mr. Wolfe. Now, you sir, tell me about your product."

"Yes, Colonel. I am Joseph Rolla. I'm Chief Technical Officer at Domestic Depot. We manufacture and sell a full line of robots designed to handle a wide range of everyday chores and responsibilities for both home and industrial markets. Included in our product line are very lifelike, handsome humanoid bots that can cook, wash, clean, change diapers on infants and adults, landscape, drive vehicles, run machinery."

"Fine, Mr. Rolla. Same question regarding memory capacity and current availability."

"Within our humanoid platforms, we can probably get away with six-hundred gigs for basic muscle activity, and another four hundred, maybe, for specialized applications and AI functionality."

Rolla smiled at Valentine, obviously pleased with himself.

"So, about a full terabyte of memory altogether. We manufacture approximately twenty units per week. That could easily be stepped up to twenty-five, or so. We generally ship them around Tartz as soon as they come off the line. We may have a dozen on the shipping docks right now."

Jack Valentine flinched, wrote something quickly, then turned to Gloria.

"Thank you, Mr. Rolla. Ma'am, what do you have for me?"

Gloria smiled, shifted in her chair, recrossed her legs provocatively.

"Well, Jack, I am Gloria Gloria and I own, run, and am CTO of BFFs HotBots. We build extremely lifelike humanoid bots designed for advanced intimacy and companionship. Our target market, our very satisfied target market, are bazillionaires who want the highest levels of sensual pleasure, obedience, imagination, and physical attractiveness that money can buy. You know, without all the complications of commitment, responsibility, and pre-nups."

"You make sex dolls?" Jack grinned.

"Our BFFs are to 'sex dolls'," smiled Gloria, "what floco is to ragweed. A whole different magnitude of experience."

"I really don't care what these bots do in their day, or night, jobs. Tell me about memory and inventory."

"Now, now, Jack, before we get into my panty drawer here, I would like for Sneezy Mike and Joe to step outside. Trade secrets, you know?"

"They showed you their panties. This is of utmost security concern. I'm sure they've reverse engineered some of your 'companions' as part of normal corporate espionage."

Jack held his palms open and gave Gloria the come-on finger wiggle.

"Give me the quick and dirty on memory and how many BFFs you have in the warehouse. I am interested, frankly, in their reaction to your claims."

"Well, I am sure if Sneezy Mike got his mitts on one of my HotBots, he did a lot more than reverse engineer. Although, reversing no doubt went on. "

Mike Wolf glared at Gloria. Clearly some history there. Of which Colonel Jack Valentine had zero interest.

"Just go on, Miss Gloria. Please."

"Okay. We only make a humanoid platform. The specs you mentioned fall easily within our standard designs. Currently, approximately two terabytes of memory are given over to our top model. Of that, about 1.2 terabytes drive the motor skills, the rest is for customized application and AI functions. And, I'd bet we currently have forty or more HotBots just waiting for some rich dude who wants to get his freak on."

Jack sat back in his chair and whistled, "Those things have eight hundred gigs of sex stuff in their processing units?"

Shrugging, Gloria said, "Well, lots of that is for standard TLC and affection. But, yeah, we try to please and many of those bazillionaires are pretty sick effers."

The lack of push back from Mike Wolf and Joe Rolla strongly suggested to Colonel Valentine that Gloria Gloria's claims to having bots whose technologies far exceeded their own products were not just puffery. He thought, "I guess the mechanical, cognitive, and AI requirements of giving an injection or washing windows were less that those required of a high-end escort."

"Thank you, Miss Gloria, anything else that you would like to add?"

"It's Mrs. Gloria. Yes, I would add that we can, within our current humanoid platforms, step up the memory max to a full four teras."

Mike Wolf piped up first.

"I just have to call BS on that one. What you're claiming is impossible, Gloria. And dangerous. This guy hasn't said it but you know we're here today because of that monster ship out there blasting away at us. Your crap and lies could get us all killed."

"Sorry, Mikey. We made a breakthrough in our chip miniaturization and sub-routine efficiencies two years ago and have just been refining them waiting for market demand to catch up. We were going to go public at the next SexCon this summer."

Joe Rolla jumped in.

"Mike's right, Colonel, she's blowing smoke up your…uniform."

Valentine turned to the intriguing Mrs. Gloria Gloria,

"Tell me, Ma'am, can you pull all the sex stuff out and add two teras and give me, say, two point eight teras of programmable capacity in fifty HotBots, and, if so, how long would that take you?"

"I can deliver in two weeks. But it's going to be expensive, very expensive. There'll be a lot of disappointed, horny bazillionaires out there."

"I'm with the government, madame, price is no object. Those horny rich guys will be fine, I'm sure."

Valentine turned to Wolf and Rolla.

"Thank you, gentlemen, for coming in. If Gloria, here, is BS-ing, we'll figure it out quickly. You can say nothing to anybody about this meeting. If you do, you will be arrested for, charged with, and, I promise you, convicted of sedition. And sent away forever to a very bad place. Got it?"

Valentine then spoke to the air.

"Peggy, please escort Mr. Wolf and Mr. Rolla to their rides, with our great appreciation for their patriotic cooperation. Gentlemen."

Peggy brusquely marched into the office, collected the two male CTOs, and hustled them away. Leaving Valentine alone with Gloria Gloria.

"Well, Gloria, I guess we're about to become best friends forever."

"That's not what my BFF stands for." She let that hang in the air.

"I figured as much. But I am a married man. And you're a married woman."

"I married for the money. I've been known to take a lover in the afternoon."

"Is Gloria Gloria your real name?"

"It's the alias that I've been living under."

Colonel Jack Valentine shook his head and laughed out loud.

"Gloria Gloria."

Chapter Three: Training Bros

Twelve days later, two large, self-driving trucks drove through the gates of a large airfield and training area about forty miles from New Baltimore. Out of either arrogance or ignorance, the Ozmonds had not bothered blasting the base, concentrating their bombardment on the power shield. Each day, Dr. Cardemone's assessment of the shield's permanency grew grimmer.

In the meantime, Colonel Valentine had Gloria Gloria checked out. She was the real deal. Gloria Uhl ran the MIT robotics research center for ten years from the incredibly young age of twenty-eight until a mutually agreed resignation. She was brilliant, transformative, charismatic and a hellish handful.

After leaving MIT, Gloria married multi-bazillionaire Elon Gloria and founded BFFs HotBot. Following three years of research and development, she rolled out her first models. They were huge sellers, even at their breathtaking price points. The hallmark of her business reputation was of someone who under-promised and over-delivered.

Colonel Jack Valentine could not have asked for a better partner for his desperate scheme to deal with the Ozmond assault in the absence of rescue from the High Consortium. As soon as Gloria's expedited security clearance was finalized, he explained his plans to her.

"I have fifty or so combat ready two-seated Corvair space fighters to go after those Ozmond bastards. The rub is I only have about five qualified pilots to fly the damn things."

Gloria chuckled.

"Let me guess. You plan to send my robotic love companions into space battle. You are crazy, Colonel. But I like it."

"My plan is to fill their pretty heads with as much tactical battle data and analytics as we can cram inside that two point eight terabytes. We have the basic tech info on the Corvair, all available actual battle records, and tons of simulator files."

Jack smiled at Gloria.

"That combined with the bots' advanced real-time AI capabilities…our guys were mightily impressed…should allow them to engage with the Ozmonds and have a fighting chance."

"What exactly is it that you want to do?"

"I want to take down that mother effing mothership. Silence those atomic rail guns, or at least chase them away until HCHQ sends some reinforcements."

"Can the space fighters take on and destroy that big mothership?"

"They'll all be carrying two hydrogen torpedoes. My tech teams have been studying super detailed images of the ship, looking for clues as to their defenses and vulnerabilities. Intel suggests that the Ozmonds shouldn't have the capabilities of that mothership. Either the Ozmonds made some quantum leap in their skills and equip or some naughty player is helping them out."

"What could they want?"

"Obviously, something to do with the floco. Either grab it and hold it until some breakthrough on the time travel thing. Or they simply want to destroy it and deny everyone else time travel. Who knows? Not my problem. My job…our job…is to defend New Baltimore and that's what I intend to do."

"Will the bots have to actually fly the Corvairs?"

"During the frontal attack, yes. They'll need to dogfight their way in, fire their two torpedoes and then haul. Each Corvair will have a cadet to fly it into position and then back home. We didn't want to waste precious memory on the basics."

"Are you going on the mission?"

"Wouldn't miss it."

Fifty shiny new HotBots were in those trucks, ready for programming and then training simulations and sorties with cadets. Jack and Gloria walked out to watch the unloading.

"Gloria, they are all naked."

Most were female, with every anatomical variant a pervert might desire. The male bots were all well-equipped.

"We don't carry flight suits in our fantasy inventory. But if this nuttiness works, we sure as hell will start."

Jack got on his communicator.

"Peggy, I need fifty medium sized scrubs from medical supplies asap to the delivery port. Better send some large pants too. Some of these toys have big toys. Thanks."

Gloria Gloria helped supervise the uploading of the flight combat data files. Her techs had stripped away the "sex stuff" from the bots but retained all the anatomical functionality and some low-level personality features.

"My guys can still play chess, tell dad jokes and win sports bar trivia contests," she told Valentine.

"Hmm, maybe I'll challenge one of these bimbos to a chess game."

"She'll kick your ass."

"A little chess knowledge might help them up there, actually."

The uplink and testing and debugging took two days, then the bots marched to the cadet assembly area to meet their new co-pilots and wingmen. The cadets had been training for the secret mission and had been given the broad outlines of the fact that their cos would be advanced humanoid robots. The cadets were so pleased to be flying Corvairs, they were fine with sharing their cockpit with a machine. What the hell, a bot is just a bucket of bolts, right?

Valentine tasked Peggy to randomly assign the bots to the cadets. She had seen the HotBots before they donned their scrubs and confirmed the male bots' prodigious attributes. She thought it wise to randomly assign them to straight male cadets, even though the cadets split about fifty-fifty between male and female.

"Where there's no temptation, there's no sinning."

Peggy was confident in her tweaking of pure randomness. Valentine noted the tweak and defaulted to Mitchell's wisdom without comment.

As the bots marched smartly into the assembly hangar, the cadets standing in rank and at attention maintained their military discipline, save for many widening eyes and gaping jaws. Colonel Valentine took to the podium.

"People, as you know, New Baltimore has been under enemy attack for weeks. Fortunately, the shielding cone has held up under relentless, high ordinance bombardment. But these attacks are so unprecedented, the scientists in charge of the shield are pretty squirmy about confidently predicting that no breach will occur."

Colonel Valentine looked out over his young, eager cadets.

"We presume significant military assistance is on the way. But it is, at best, still several days away. This unit is the only viable countering armed force on Tartz to meet the current emergency. We can stay here and pray the shield holds. Or we can go take those bastards down. I say, we're going to go get those Ozmond pricks and make them regret ever coming at Tartz.'"

Despite their military training and discipline, the cadets broke into cheering and clapping, whistling and Rebel yells. The bots watched the cadets and, by God, they started cheering and whistling too. Gloria, standing to the side, smiled.

"These bots are your best new pals. They used to be in the companionship business. Now they're in the Ozmond snuffing business. As a team, you and one of these bots will fly a fully armed Corvair. We will engage that mothership and the counter measures they will throw at us. All of the in-close air combat, all the dive attacks with hydrogen torpedoes, all the dog-fighting will be handled by your bot co-pilot."

A murmur of griping and angry questioning roiled through the cadets, in spite of their military bearing. They were not happy cadets.

Colonel Valentine let the pot boil and simmer for a long moment, then barked, "Knock it off. These guys have every bite of air combat knowledge within the High Consortium's files in their pretty heads. The hard truth is, they are right now far better fighter pilots than any of you. Any of you."

Valentine was all no nonsense as he pressed on.

"Some of you think you're pretty hot shot. I'm telling you none of you pretty hot shots could take any of these HotBots. Maybe, someday, through training, practice, and experience you will be their equal. Today you're raw, untried, and full of misguided confidence. These sex dolls would light up any of you in a doggie."

Gloria walked over and whispered in Valentine's ear. He looked out at the cadets.

"I will be leading this attack and I'll have a bot in the pit with me. And I'll be relying on that co-pilot. I've forgotten more about air-to-air combat since breakfast than most of you will know after twenty years of service."

The Colonel held up two fingers.

"Two final things before you meet your best new pal. One, the bots have been programmed to place your survival above the mission. That priority can only be reversed by me. Two: You're young, you're arrogant, you're horny. Keep your mitts off your co-pilot. Any breach of that order will be handled harshly with court-martial and prison."

One last steely glare.

"Make Tartz proud. I'll see you in three short days and we'll go trolling for Ozmonds. Dismissed."

And for three mean days, the cadets practiced hard with their new crewmates. The Corvair was already loaded with plenty of computing power, but the human pilots soon realized that the fighter's capabilities were significantly enhanced by the crackerjack brains of the humanoids. The bots were also found to have the physical dexterity and pure athleticism of a professional tennis player, with unlimited energy. And their AI grasp and command was incredible. These humanoids seldom made a mistake in the real and simulated training exercises. They never made the same mistake twice.

Perhaps the most impressive bot quality to the cadets was the personality and companionship of the humanoids. That they were designed and programmed to become each human pilot's best friend forever was recognized by the humans, but the damn bots were so good at it, no one cared. They were great company. Funny, smart, attractive, and empathetic. No pilot doubted that their bot co-pilot was fully dedicated to the mission and the survival of their human.

Jack Valentine's co-pilot was a comely, small chested blonde named Marcie. Gloria Gloria and Peggy had clearly conspired on this random assignment. Instead of the scrubs worn by other HotBots, Marcie wore fashionable high wasted slacks, a white blouse with small hearts and heart shaped buttons and a chic bolo jacket. As Gloria explained to the Colonel, Marcie was dressed for Valentine's.

Chapter Four: Mother Effing Mothership

After intense surveillance and high-level flybys of the Ozmond mothership by small, space drones, the space force strategists, assisted by MIT engineers, developed a plan of attack. The mothership was a standard inter-galactic dreadnaught, probably pirated by the Ozmonds within the last twenty years. Deep Research found records of five such beasts that had gone missing during that period and were confident they had the original schematics of the Ozmond ship.

The most obvious target for hydrogen torpedoes was at a juncture of bulkheads tucked in behind the starboard railgun. According to the original ship plans, vital control and command systems and the main bridge lie there. The exterior fortifications and the added structural integrity of the massed bulkheads were formidable. Valentine's team were confident that the walls could be pierced and mortal fire delivered internally assuming approximately twenty torpedoes accurately struck within a thirty square meter target near the bulkhead joint. This was designated Target Alpha.

Target Beta was the secondary target 180 degrees aft of Target Alpha. Backup power resources and the ship's atomic ordinance armory were here. Valentine's think tank did not believe that a full-on successful attack here would bring the ship down. But a successful attack should paralyze the ship and destroy its ability to continue the bombardment of New Baltimore. Colonel Valentine wanted to kill the mothership.

The third possible point of attack, Target Gamma, was a point on the ship's underbelly that the original blueprints indicated had relatively thin protection from torpedo attack. Classic soft underbelly. Nothing down there except crew's quarters and non-ordinance warehousing. A concentrated attack there might pierce the exterior shielding and allow torpedoes to find their way destructively into the ship's interior. But, unless several dozen torpedoes actually blasted well into the ship, mission planners did not believe that the mothership would be rendered inoperative. The ship might have a hard time escaping eventual destruction, but it could continue its barrage as a kamikaze mission. Valentine was seriously no fan of Target Gamma.

On the morning of the fourth day following the cadets' introduction to their robotic co-pilots, Colonel Jack Valentine addressed the assembled crews again. He stood in front of a large hologram of the alien mothership.

"People and…HotBots…you have all been briefed on the mission that will commence immediately. This is Alpha Target. This is where we'll concentrate our fire. We need at least two dozen bogies to hit this small target area, break down their walls and take out their entire command and control capabilities. With luck, the result should be the ship losing its orbital integrity and falling into Turtle. We have one hundred torpedoes in our attack group. Given the formidable resistance we expect to encounter, we face a high hit ratio goal. I am confident this attack group will succeed in this vital mission."

Colonel Valentine looked at his young squadron. Their faces and body-language brimmed with eagerness and self-confidence. Hell, the bots had more grownup concern on their plastic faces than the cadets had on their human mugs. How many of these ramped up kids will be alive tomorrow? Jack sighed. He loved them all and was enormously proud.

He flipped the hologram around.

"This is Beta Target. If I, or a successor commander, order a cessation of attack at Target Alpha, fight your way immediately into position to torpedo attack here. Again, we probably need twenty to twenty-five bullseyes to break through and destroy their big ammo. We don't get to go all the way, but we get to third base."

The cadets and bots chuckled.

"Here is Target Gamma," Valentine flipped the hologram to show the ship's bottom and keel, "down in the ship's bilge. If Alpha and Beta are no-gos, we attack here. If we must, we will. This isn't even like getting to second base, this is like kissing your own sibling. With no tongue."

More chuckles. Valentine thought them ready, if ever that was possible.

"Okay, we'll fly in picket formation, with cadets piloting. It'll take approximately six hours to our designated assembly point for the attack on Target Alpha. There, the bots will take command of each Corvair and we'll attack as per your assigned priorities. After firing your torpedoes, return to the assembly point and prepare to escort other fighters if needed."

Cadets nodded. The bots then also nodded.

"That said, you will most likely have to fight your way into torpedo launch point then back out again. Stay engaged if your squadron fellows need help. I want to see you all back here for a victory breakfast tomorrow. I love you all. Now let's go."

The squadron flew to the attack assembly point. They met no resistance from marauding fighters patrolling far from the mothership. Valentine's mission planners believed the anti-fighter cannons on the mothership were of little use at the distance of the attack assembly point. The lack of resistance was not wholly surprising but still struck Valentine as quirky. He would have sent harassing sorties of fighters just to mess with the Corvairs. Maybe they had too few to spare.

From their pre-attack vantage they could see the enormous command battleship and the mammoth railguns firing nuclear ordinance at their family, friends, and homes. All fifty Corvair crews were ready to bring the fight to the Ozmonds.

"First wing, begin your attack," Valentine ordered. "Second wing, wait for my command."

Five Corvairs on the formation's right flank dove at the mothership. Immediately ten anti-fighter cannons, known to them from intelligence photos, began firing at the first wing. Five hidden, unknown cannons swung out of the mothership's hull surrounding Alpha Target and blasted away at the Corvairs. Almost immediately, two of the Tartzian fighters were obliterated by cannon fire.

"Damnit," hissed Valentine.

The formidable AI functionality of the bots commanding the other three Corvairs instantly adjusted to the fifteen cannons and they swept in at dizzying speed and maneuvering to their torpedo launch distance and fired. Six torpedoes blasted into the mothership's bulkhead exactly where the mission planners had designated. The surviving fighters of first wing returned to position at right flank.

Valentine heard cheers through the inter-squadron intercom. The Colonel mourned the loss of the two Corvair crews. He was impressed by the bots' piloting. But the attack seemed too easy, despite the forty percent mortality rate. He needed to get a hands-on feel.

"Second wing, prepare to attack. On my lead."

To his bot co-pilot, on the fighter's intercom, Valentine said, "Marcie, stand down, I'll take combat command here."

"Yes sir. One suggestion: Kasparov Blue Feint."

"Say again, Marcie."

"Kasparov Blue Feint, Sir."

The Kasparov Blue Feint was a storied chess stratagem employed by Garry Kasparov several hundred years earlier in the first sanctioned match between a reigning chess champion and a supercomputer known as Deep Blue. Kasparov prevailed in the first of a six-game match by using a double trap feint.

He set up a semi-disguised trap that suckered Deep Blue into attacking for a quick mate. Once the computer recognized the trap, it switched to a different line of attack. The new attack was suggested by Blue's position and would have eventually led to Kasparov's forced retirement. EXCEPT, that was a trap too. By the move Deep Blue finally realized the second trap, the computer's position was so disadvantaged, it had to concede to Kasparov.

Colonel Valentine paused and considered Marcie's suggestion. His disquiet at the relative ease with which the attack squadron had moved into position and launched a successful first sortie, gave him pause.

"Second wing, stand down for now. I'll get back to you. All other attack wings stand ready to boogey on my orders."

Valentine called mission control in New Baltimore. He spoke to the top strategist and lead MIT engineer.

"I need to know pronto if the command-and-control elements and bridge of that damn mothership could be repositioned and a fake, torpedo eating bullet trap built at Target Alpha?"

"Sir, are you going to withdraw and wait for us to analyze this possibility."

"Now. I want an answer now. I have no intention of withdrawing."

"Fine, sir. Give us an hour or so."

"You have thirty minutes."

Valentine hoped the Ozmonds would believe the attack delay was because they knew that cadets with little or no combat experience were in the Corvairs and that they were unnerved by four of their number getting killed. Twenty-seven minutes after calling mission control, Jack heard back.

"We had a little luck, Colonel. In the files for the dreadnaught prototype of what we believe is the mothership up there, other engineers have played with the hypothetical reconfiguration you suggest. We took that and added the bullet trap notion you also suggested."

"Get to it," barked Valentine.

"Ah, yes sir. The remodel you suggest is possible, if not likely."

"Why is it not likely?"

"Ah, well mostly, because it never occurred to us."

"I appreciate your honesty. Where would you reposition the command and control if it had occurred to you to do so?"

"Actually, per the hypotheticals, they would be positioned under the ship."

"Near Target Gamma?"

"Directly behind Target Gamma."

"Thank you, ten-four."

Valentine hopped back on the squad intercom.

"Okay, here's what I want. Bots, you stay in command. I want the appearance of an organized retreat to Tartz, starting with a left flank pullback. Tenth flight, when you have withdrawn two hundred klicks from your current holding position, turn around, dive low, and torpedo the hell out of Target Gamma. Expect high resistance, including fighter intercept. All other flights follow ten."

One wag cadet chirped, "This mean I have to kiss my brother?"

Valentine smiled and said, "We are going for full-on, hard taboo, incest. Good luck."

Tenth flight, off the left side of the holding position, banked and proceeded to appear heading back to base. The other flights followed suit, giving the appearance of an organized withdrawal. Then the lead Corvairs reversed course and pounced at the bottom of the huge mothership.

The Ozmonds were caught with their pants, or whatever they wore, down. Tenth flight dove straight onto Target Gamma and precisely delivered their torpedoes. Ninth flight were right on their tails but, by then, ten previously hidden anti-fighter cannons emerged from the ship's hull and began blasting. Then dozens of

Ozmond fighters emerged from over the top of the mothership and engaged the Corvairs in a massive dogfight.

Valentine ordered his fighters to break ranks and do whatever necessary to deliver their torpedoes, then rejoin the dogfight and "smash those killer hornets."

Valentine was having a hell of a time dodging cannon flak and Ozmond fighters. His Corvair had obviously been identified as the command bird and he was getting way too much attention.

Marcie spoke, "Sir, with respect, would you like for me to take it from here?"

Marcie's AI had been absorbing all the new intel from the battle raging. Valentine was neither prideful nor stupid.

"Your stick, Marcie."

With that, Valentine's fighter dove straight down at full speed, creating g-force in excess of the cockpit gravity countering technology of the Corvair. Valentine passed out.

When the Colonel came to, he and Marcie were well off from the intense dogfighting under the mothership. Valentine checked his battle data dashboard. Twelve Corvairs lost in the fight. Twenty-two torpedoes struck the target but the mothership stood firm. The railguns continued to fire.

Before he could order Marcie to rejoin the battle, Peggy popped through on his command communicator.

"I'm kinda busy up here, Mitchell."

"Yes, Sir. Just heard from Cardemone. The shield is unraveling. Don't know how much longer we can hold out. City residents are in full panic, trying to evacuate to the country."

"Damn it. Damn it."

Right on cue, the rail guns quit firing and the huge mothership began to, no other word, tremble.

Valentine shouted into the squad intercom, "Corvairs, get the hell out of there now. Beat it. Full speed."

Valentine's battle dashboard showed thirty-two Tartzian Corvairs dashing away from the dogfight. Some of the enemy fighters gave chase at first but then realized the dire situation of their mothership and fell back.

Valentine ordered his squad to reassemble around his position. He still had thirty-two Corvairs, most were damaged. Among them were eight unfired torpedoes. Valentine positioned the seven fighters with a torpedo behind the other twenty-five Corvairs. If the mothership steadied itself and began firing again on New Baltimore, he was prepared to blast his way back to Target Gamma and deliver those last torpedoes.

The mothership appeared to recover some stability and began to re-engage its railguns. As Valentine readied to order a last desperate attack, three massive dreadnaught battleships popped into the starry sky above the mothership. Each flew the colors of the High Consortium and each fired their massive guns simultaneously. The Ozmond mothership disintegrated into powder. The destruction was so massive that the Corvairs barely felt a ripple from their standing position.

Valentine spoke to his cadets and HotBots.

"You all were magnificent. Battle commanders, return your fighters to the command of the cadets and carefully make your way home. If your fighter is too wounded to get home, have one of those calvary monsters give you a lift. Your com channels are being monitored by them, so just holler."

Valentine's com speaker crackled and a voice came through.

"This is Admiral Kuhr of the HC Battle Fleet Group. We have been monitoring your heroic stand and could not be prouder of your fine cadets. And…ah, your volunteers. Sorry it took us so long to ride in. Glad to help, though it looked like you had it won, Colonel."

"Thank you, Admiral. We appreciate your help."

"Fine, I'll see you all down on Tartz. And I want to meet someone named Peggy Mitchell. Never really had a junior officer tell me to move my ass before. "

Epilog

Three weeks after the Battle of Tartz, General Jack Valentine was sitting at his desk when Colonel Peggy Mitchell opened the office door and stepped aside as Admiral Kuhr marched in."

Valentine immediately stood and saluted.

Kuhr returned the salute.

"Sit down, Jack. I should be saluting you. This whole planet should be saluting you."

"Thank you, Sir. Many people, and other beings, contributed to the effort. Wasn't only me."

"Well, it was you that safely evacuated those moons and conscripted the sexbots. It was you who used some ancient chess gambit to see through the Ozmond's ruse. No, if they ever bring back Valentine's Day…and I sure as hell hope they don't…it should be in your honor. You saved a city of forty million from certain destruction and you saved the floco."

"Just doing the job, Sir. "

"I was just doing my job, negotiating with that Gloria Gloria. We want to keep those comely fighter aces you pressed into service. She wants a boodle, which we'll gladly pay. She also informed me that she takes lovers in the afternoon."

"Yes, sir, good luck with that."

"She's not my type. But that little Peggy vixen in the outer office…if it wasn't forbidden."

"You do know, Admiral, she can hear you."

'Yeah, I know. I'm retiring soon. What the hell?"

"Any news on what the Ozmonds were doing or how they had such advanced technology and weaponry."

"It's a conundrum, Jack. The Ozmond Conundrum. We'll track it all down. Got our suspicions. You sure you don't want to transfer to HCHQ? Could be fun."

"I'm fine here, Admiral, with the bedwetters. Thanks."

Jack's hologram pinged and Marcy appeared wearing only three very strategically placed but very small Tartzian flags.

"Hey, General, wanna be a good patriot and come home? I could use a tall flagpole."

"Marcy, I'm chatting in high top secret with Admiral Kuhr."

"Oh. Hi Admiral. Nice to see you again."

"Marcy, you are looking very patriotic. Jack's lucky to have such a gung-ho, foxhole mate."

"Did you say fox hole, Admiral?"

Jack reached for the hologram remote.

"Goodbye, Marcy. See you at home."

Ping.

Alfa Romeo, R.I.P.

Notable Author: John DeDakis (Sept 2020)

Genre: Mystery/Suspense
Prompt: Use up to 100 words and write a mystery/suspense piece centered around journalism.

Prompt Forward

Detective GK Hardace ducked under the crime scene tape and strolled toward his partner Maria White who was standing next to a shot out Alfa Romeo. A bloody, messy corpse slumped over the steering wheel.

Hardace nodded to White.

"Who's the scrambled eggs in the Jag?"

"Alfa Romeo. The deceased is…was…Johnny Lessen, the TV guy."

"Never heard of him."

"Hard to believe, GK, you're such a with-it guy. Lessen fancied himself an investigative journalist, kind of a down-market Geraldo, only slimier."

Hardace grunted, "Go on."

"He ruined lotsa lives, many needlessly. Got ratings cause people love to hate him. I didn't know the weasel and I hated him. Most people will think the murder of the Alfa is the tragedy here. We won't have any shortage of motivated suspects on this one."

GK turned to leave.

"Well, put your gumshoes on Maria. I'll get his phone and computer records. See you back at the office and you can tell me who-the-hell Geraldo is."

Chapter One: KYJY-TV

GK Hardace wasn't as clueless as he would sometimes let on. He knew who Johnny Lessen was. A two-bit scandal-chaser who'd been doing dirt on Pittsburgh's KYJY-TV for years, decades probably. Lessen wasn't GK's cup of anything.

Hardace knew human nature if he knew nothing else. People love the misery of other folks; helps them cope with their own woe. Lessen traded in schadenfreude, and probably made a pretty good living at it. He could afford to drive one of those high-priced German Jags.

Hardace agreed with Maria's quick take that motivated suspects would be no problem in this case.

Lessen's laptop and phone were in his car next to his rotting remains. Whoever iced him wasn't interested in them. Neither his laptop nor phone were password or bio protected. GK loved Luddites. Tech was able to categorize gigabytes of data and info. The devices were at the scene of the crime, so they were fair game for law enforcement. Hardace was mostly interested in recent e-mails, phone calls and text messages and GPS records on Lessen's phone. God bless Steve Jobs.

The deceased Alfa was impounded as evidence in the police holding lot. Lessen's perforated corpse was shipped to the morgue for autopsy (death by multiple gun shots to key organs, but his liver was going to kill him soon anyhow. His blood alcohol level was .22). His earthly remains were delivered
to a funeral home for some spackling and a quickie funeral. Lessen's nearest relative was a brother who hated his guts and made no secret of the fact that he was glad Lessen was dead.

"Bout time," Larry Lessen told the press, "If I had any guts, I'd have done it myself years ago. "

Larry then smartly lawyered up, shut up and took care of the funeral arrangements. Lessen's quick send-off was the first celebrity funeral in Pittsburgh since the death of a defrocked Archbishop whose affection for altar boys was legendary, and expensive.

People booed and spat at Lessen's short funeral cortege as it made its way through the South Side. Johnny Lessen was buried in Allegheny Cemetery, an honor he shared along with 120,000 other departed Pittsburghians. His grave quickly became a urine puddle. Bonum est faciet.

While Lessen's cadaver was being remanded to Allegheny Cemetery's slatey soil, Detectives GK Hardace and Maria White were on the trail of his murderer. Hardace, whose nickname among Pittsburgh's finest was, no surprise, "hardass" took every murder investigation personally. He believed he owed the victims some measure of justice, even a puke like Johnny Lessen.

Hardace told Maria, "I'm not sure whoever did it is going to prison or is going to be Rotary's Man of Year, or both."

GK's and Maria's first call was to Lessen's long-term employer, KYJY-TV. They stepped into Station Manager Dennis Noble's office at nine am, two days after Lessen's body was found in his new Alfa Romeo behind a defunct strip mall. They had no appointment and if Noble had some administrative assistant type who was supposed to guard his door, that person was AWOL.

A middle-aged white guy wearing expensive office casual clothes and a silly haircut looked at the two detectives.

"Uhhh…what do you want?"

GK took the lead, "Are you Dennis Noble?"

Maria's first thought was that punctuation matters. Maybe GK asked, "Are you, Dennis, noble?"

The man behind the desk responded with little nobility.

"Who the hell are you two?"

Hardace and White flashed their PPD badges and introduced themselves.

"We're here, "deadpanned Hardace, "investigating the murder of your late employee, Johnny Lessen."

Dennis Noble shrugged, "That prick."

Maria White calmly asked, "Did you want to kill him?"

"Many times."

Hardace arched his eyebrows, "Did you kill him?"

"No, some other civic-minded citizen beat me to it."

"Doggone, I thought we were going to get this cleared up in time for me to see Kelly and Ryan. Well, Dennis, since you claim you didn't kill Mr. Lessen, when was the last time you saw him?"

"Probably the day he was shot."

"How do you know he was shot," Hardace asked.

"I read the newspapers, Detective, you might want to try it."

Maria pulling, as ever, good cop duty spoke up,

"Whoa, Dennis…may I call you Dennis…we just want to ask you a few questions about Lessen, any problems or threats he might have experienced as part of his job. That kind of thing."

Noble picked up his desk phone and pushed a button.

"Harvey? Yeah, Dennis here. Come down to my office. A couple of cops here asking about the late, unlamented Lessen. Thanks."

Hardace and White looked at each other and shrugged.

"Your attorney?"

"Yeah. Harvey Katz. He hated Lessen too."

A very professional lawyer-type entered the office, expensive suit, and crisp hair. Introductions were made. Katz took a seat next to Hardace and White.

Hardace began.

"Let's just cut to the chase. Everyone seems to have hated this guy. Why did you keep him around?"

Noble shrugged.

"Once, Johnny delivered great numbers. He had a Saturday night show, which is usually poison for local, non-sport, programming. Even his demos were good. Young dudes and dudettes watched him as much as the oldsters. He tossed dirt, carefully vetted by Harvey Katz, dirt on locals. He didn't care if they were Mellons or trash living in a double-wide in Point Merion. Viewers out there in TV land would pop an Iron City and watch to see if someone they knew had drifted into Lessen's crosshairs."

"You said 'once delivered.' Were his numbers no longer great," asked Maria.

"His ratings had slipped. A lot. Our market research showed that the demand was still there for dirt. Many people had just got tired of Lessen. He'd worn out his welcome in Pittsburgh. We were getting ready to make a change."

"Did he know that?"

"I told him the day he got croaked."

GK looked directly at Noble.

"What exactly did you tell Lessen?"

"Just what I told you. Crashing numbers. Bad E.Q. We were not going to renew his contract. Going to give his protégé Tina Harman the job. Probably change the name of the show from 'Hard Lessen' to 'Hard Harman.'"

"How'd Lessen take the news?"

"Like a bat with explosive diarrhea. Like Johnny effin Lessen. He called Tina every name in the H.R. manual that requires immediate dismissal. He threatened to sue. Violate his non-compete agreement. Blah, blah, blah. Harvey was here, he can tell you."

For the first time, Katz spoke.

"He was an a-hole. Total meltdown. On-air talent are often prima-donna douchebags. Johnny was the Baryshnikov of douchebags. We expected a crapstorm. He did not let us down."

Maria looked at Katz.

"Since everybody everywhere seems to have disliked…hated…the guy, was there anyone here on staff who would have benefited tangibly by his death?"

"No. Not really. Tina got her promotion two months early with Johnny dying. She may have suspected that she'd be moving up and Johnny moving out. But we had told no one, including her, about our plans."

"If she did know, or suspect, with Johnny still being around, publicly blasting her as only he could, probably dragging her into any lawsuits, maybe even competing against her, her transition would be easier with him dead."

Noble piped up.

"All our lives are better with him dead."

"Dennis, "Katz coughed, "I'll take any further questions unless I specifically okay you to answer. Hear me?"

Dennis Noble sheepishly nodded.

"Anyone else who might have benefited enough from Lessen kicking, to be tempted?"

"No. It's a ridiculous notion. Jack was here for almost thirty years. People hated him, for sure, but mostly they just walked around him. He did his thing with a small production crew, headed by Tina. He treated them terribly but they long ago accommodated themselves to him. Somebody here who really wanted to murder Johnny Lessen would have done so before now."

Hardace nodded.

"Was he working on any recent or current case, story, whatever you call it that was potentially dangerous? Fatally dangerous? Did he get death threats?"

Katz and Noble looked at each other and cackled in unison.

"Johnny Lessen got more death threats…phone threats, letters, e-mails, social media postings…than the President. He carried a gun, legally. He was attacked, wounded, hospitalized many times. He loved their hate."

Katz shook his head and smiled a tiny smile.

"Anytime he could broadcast from a hospital room, he'd do it. And it wasn't just new stories that drove threats. He'd get threats today from stories long ago. He ruined lives literally. Those targeted folks seldom forget, and they never forgive."

"Do you have records of these threats?"

Katz again. "We have files and files of them. They were like trophies to Jack. He made sure he kept every one."

Opening a manilla folder, Hardace extracted some papers.

"From his phone and GPS records, we see that in the past few weeks he has made almost thirty calls to different numbers in Moundsville, West Virginia. Also, his phone GPS records show that he had visited Moundsville at least three times in the weeks before his murder. That little car he was killed in doesn't have a nav system so we cannot determine if that was how he got to Moundsville."

Again, Katz and Noble looked at each other. Katz spoke.

"That damn Alfa Romeo. If he went to Moundsville, he drove there in the Alfa. He was a fool for that Italian piece of crap."

"Was it a company car. Would he have filed for some expense reimbursement for milage, listing justification for the trip?"

"No, I'm sure he did not add Moundsville trips to his expense claims. He had been ordered, by me, to not pursue any story in Moundsville. These calls and trips were not sanctioned by KYJY-TV. Had we known about the Moundsville stuff, we would have fired him for insubordination. On the spot."

"What's so special about Moundsville?"

Katz sighed and looked at Hardace.

"I'd like to say Moundsville has nothing to do with your murder case. Who-the-hell knows? Johnny was not beloved in Moundsville. He was dumb to go there, especially in that ridiculous car. What a fool."

GK again. "What's so special about Moundsville?"

Harvey Katz turned to Noble and nodded.

"I wasn't here then. Dennis, go ahead and tell the detectives about Johnny Lessen and Moundsville, West Virginia."

Chapter Two: Moundsville, West Virginia

Dennis Noble sat back in his desk chair, rubbed his brow, and began.

"About ten years ago, several of the Moundsville High School football team had a late summer party to celebrate the new season. Moundsville High was a football powerhouse and were the defending state champions. High school football was about all Moundsville had going for it.

GK asked," What is Moundsville? I know it's on the Ohio River, got a prison. Why's it called Moundsville. Is that like mons Venus?"

White shot Hardace a look.

"Knock it off, GK, you ass. It's from the old Indian burial mounds there. Sorry, Dennis, go ahead. I think I remember where you're going here."

"Anyway, at this party, a couple of star-struck freshman girls got drunk, fell unconscious, and were abused and mistreated by several of the football players. Pretty rank stuff. Other students video-taped all that crap, put it up on social-media. Some in real time. All bad juju."

Hardace nodded, "I kinda remember this too."

Noble nodded and continued.

"Anyway, the school and local cops got involved. The two girls and their parents just wanted it to go away. Nobody wanted the players punished. Naturally, the main a-holes in the videos were the team's star seniors. There was some local outrage, but the town just sucked it up and let the hubbub die down."

"Then someone anonymously sent Lessen one of the videos," Katz sighed.

"Yep," agreed Noble.

"Lessen got that and ran with it. Hard. Took a camera crew down there. Ambush interviewed the football coach, the principal, the police chief, the girls' parents, everybody. Stirred up a hornet's nest, then came back here and did three shows on the Moundsville mess. The whole thing went viral, then national."

Katz again, "It got huge."

Dennis Noble picked up the story.

"A woman from 'New Yorker Magazine' wrote a scorching article about America's rape culture, the misogynism of football, etc. All encapsulated by the terrible town of Moundsville. The out-of-town outrage eventually led to the high school football program being shut down, three of the star players being convicted of felony charges and going to prison, the poor girls getting dozens of death threats."

Maria White asked, "And Lessen?"

"Oh, hell, Lessen was a pig in slop. Got interviewed on all the national morning shows. '60 Minutes.' Everyone wanted Johnny Lessen for fifteen minutes. The lady from 'New Yorker' got a Pulitzer. Lessen got an Emmy and a Peabody. Moundsville got screwed. You want suspects, Detectives, there is a whole town in West Virginia full of them."

Hardace this time, "And what was Lessen's current interest in Moundsville?"

Harvey Katz put his hand on Noble's shoulder and answered.

"Johnny probably knew he was on thin ice here at the station. His ratings had cratered. He needed a hail-Mary pass. He wanted to go back down to Moundsville, do a ten year later kind of thing. He claimed that he had info about hazing and other naughty high school stuff down there. He was told, by me, absolutely not. Dennis and I sent him an e-mail very specifically and strongly ordering him to leave Moundsville the-hell alone."

"Wouldn't it have made good TV?" White wondered.

"We were sure Jack had nothing. He was just going to create a crap-storm down there, maybe get beat-up or shot at. Just scratch off an old scab for no better reason than to try and save his dying career. We can be shameless in our chasing ratings. But we do have some standards."

Katz then jumped in.

"And we don't need senseless, probably expensive, litigation over some high school kids acting like jackasses. That's hardly cutting-edge journalism."

Hardace and White stood up.

"Looks like Lessen wasn't heeding your orders and warnings. We'll track that down. Thank you for your time this morning."

"That it?" Katz wondered.

"For now. We'll have more questions, I'm sure. We will be speaking to Miss Harman. If she wants you there Mr. Katz, we can't object, but she should hire her own attorney. Must be some kind of conflict of interest in there somewhere."

Katz was droll, "Thank you for the legal advice, Detective Hardace,"

"You're welcome."

Detectives Hardace and White went to leave. They shook hands with Noble and Katz. As they left Noble's office, Hardace turned and directed a question to Noble.

"One last thing, Mr. Noble. I've always been curious about this, KYJY-TV has been around a long time, right?"

"We are the third oldest broadcaster in the United States," beamed Noble.

"So, the whole town calls you KY-Jelly. Have you ever thought about changing your call letters?"

Katz and Noble looked at each other with stony faces and said nothing.

"Okay, "shrugged Hardace, "just wondering."

He and Detective White closed the door behind themselves.

Chapter Three: Suspects

GK shrugged, "I guess they've heard that before."

"You think?" White spit. "You can be a horse's ass."

"I try. Let's go back to the office. You get out that smart phone of yours and Googleate and find the name and number of the Police Chief, or Sheriff, or the High Constable or whoever runs The Moundsville LE."

Detectives Hardace and White got back to 1203 Western in seven minutes and retired to Holdace's small, glass enclosed office. They called the Moundsville Police Department Chief Thomas Mason. Their call was intercepted by a Teresa Spero, Administrative Aide.

"How can I help you?"

"Hey, Ms. Spero, this is Detective GK Hardace from the Pittsburgh Police Department. Detective Maria White and I would just like a few minutes of Captain Mason's time to chat about a case we got up here. Is he available?"

"Detective Hardass, you say?"

"Hardace. Just a few minutes of Captain Mason's precious time would be grand." Hardace rolled his eyes at White.

Teresa Spero was no fool.

"How do I know this call is legitimate? How do I know this isn't just some clownfish down at the Moose? I know you dog turds. You sound like Timmy Carter."

"Ma'am, don't you have caller id down there in Moundsville? Let me give you my number, get on our web site, check us out. Have Captain Mason call us back if he won't mind. Reverse the charges. We don't give a crap. A little professional courtesy, please."

Hardace gave her his direct line and hung up.

Maria White cocked an eyebrow. "You are a diplomatic bastard. Henry Kissinger would be proud."

Hardace shrugged, "Screw 'em if they can't take a joke."

Twenty-two minutes later, Captain Tom Mason returned Hardace's call.

"Detective Hardace, how can I be of service to Pittsburgh's finest? Used to work there myself, twenty-some years ago. Great memories."

"Captain Mason, thanks for calling back. Got you on speaker with Detective Maria White. We're calling about the murder of a Pittsburgh fellow named Johnny Lessen."

Mason snorted.

"You want a contribution to the killer's legal fund. I can get you a bundle down here. The whole Department will kick in, starting with me."

"Well, we haven't caught the hero yet. Thought maybe you could help us with that."

"Fire away, Detective."

"We can see from Lessen's personal records that he made several calls to Moundsville recently. A call to your office was the longest one. Also, he drove down there at least three times in the past few weeks. You talk to him lately?"

"Sure did. He called. Wanted to talk about all that crap from ten years ago. Said he might have info about some new mischief out there with the MHS football team."

"You believe him?"

"Oh, hell no. The high school just got football back again a few years ago. They have a good shot this year. We and the school keep a close eye on the program. My boy plays on the team. Everything is super kosher over there. You can take that to the bank."

"You tell that to Lessen?"

"You bet I did. He said I was as corrupt as Chief Baker, my predecessor who was chief back when. He said he had proof, was going to blow the roof off a hazing scandal, more rape parties. BS like that."

Hardace coughed, "What'd you say?"

"I told him to drop it. Nothing there. If he came to town looking to stir up that pot again, the local citizenry, and the local law enforcement would be most unwelcoming."

"That scare him off."

"Of course not. He started screaming about the First Amendment. No tin badge was going to scare him off from doing the job of 'shining a light on the cockroaches of corruption.' His words."

"He come see you?"

"Tried to. He burst in a few days later, drove down here in that sissy car. He had no appointment, tried to barge past Miss Spero into my office. Had some gal filming it all."

"What happen?"

"Well, Miss Spero, God bless her, is a big old river gal and she laid a chop block on him would have made Gerry Mullins proud. I came out and saw him lying on the floor like roadkill and told him to get the hell out and stay out. The little gal filming the whole thing was laughing like a fool, but she kept that camera rolling."

"Did he ever come back?"

"Nah, not here. He came back to town a couple of times. Tried the same crap with the football coach, the principal, even the parents of the gals from last time. My understanding is he got the same cold shoulder from those folks, maybe not with the Miss Spero emphasis."

Mason chuckled again at the memory.

"But he got nowhere with anyone down here. That car announced his stink wherever he went, and Moundsville ignored him. Lucky he didn't get shot down here first. The town might want to buy that wuss car and put it out front of the American Legion next to the little tank."

"The car's as dead as Lessen," Maria White said.

"That's a shame. He got nothing here, cause there was nothing to get. He clearly was trying to create a hubbub where there was none to be had. Nobody here is sorry he's dead."

Hardace asked, "If you had to point a finger or two at some locals, could you? Would you?"

"Nothing here, Detective." Tom Mason was very emphatic. "Nothing."

"Okay, Chief, thanks for your help. We owe you a T-bone if you ever get to the 'Burgh." Hardace hung up.

"What do you think?" GK asked Maria.

"My gut tells me that Moundsville is a dead end. Like the Chief said, Lessen didn't seem to get anywhere. He was going to have to create outrage out of very thin air. Whoever whacked him seemed pretty hot and angry. Just seems like the motivation had to be more current."

"I agree. Funny how everyone hated that car of Lessen's. Silly. Okay, set up a meet with that Tina chick from the TV station."

"Harman"

"What'd you say, Maria?"

"Harman. Her name is Tina Harman. Not Tina 'chick.'"

Hardace shook his head, "Whatever, set up a sit down."

The next day at ten in the morning, Tina Harman and her little posse came into GK Hardace's small office and sat on some hastily collected cop chairs. Accompanying Tina was Harvey Katz and another crisp lawyerly type who introduced himself as Marc Solomon, personal attorney to Ms. Harman.

Tina Harman was a tall, slender, blonde woman, probably on the far side of thirty, but not too far. She was wearing a sleek, fashionable pantsuit and no wedding ring. She radiated self-assurance.

After introductions, GK turned to Harman.

"So, Tina, did you murder Johnny Lessen?"

Harman put up her hand to stop Solomon from objecting.

"I did not kill that horrid man, though I dreamt about doing so every day for the past seven years."

"That seems to be the basic attitude of everybody who knew the bastard. Agatha Christie would have loved this guy."

Harman shrugged, "Well, I sure didn't love the guy."

Maria White leaned in. "When was the last time you saw Johnny Lessen?"

"The day he was waxed. At work."

GK and Maria looked at each other. "Waxed."

"Did you see him after work?"

This time Harman looked to Attorney Solomon.

"You don't have to answer any questions that you don't want to answer. We are here as a curtesy to the Detectives. If you are uncomfortable, we can leave, make them get a subpoena."

"No, I'm fine," Harman smiled, "as a matter of fact I did see Johnny Lessen after work that day."

GK's eyes widened.

"Ms. Harman, if we were to subpoena your phone's GPS records"...Hardace shot a look at Solomon. "If we were to do so, would they show that you were at a derelict strip mall in Munhall that evening?"

Solomon jumped in." Tina, I think we should maybe let the good law enforcement folks have their fantasies and take our leave."

Harvey Katz jumped in. "I agree, Tina, this is getting too accusatory. Let these guys go fishing elsewhere."

Tina Harman never lost her smile. "It's okay, boys, I got this."

She turned and looked directly at Detective Hardace.

"My GPS record would most likely confirm that my telephone was at the Henry Street Shopping Center for about ten minutes that evening."

"Just your phone?" asked Detective White.

"Oh, I was there also."

"Was Lessen there too?"

"He was there. He was snot-faced drunk. He was alive when I drove away."

"How'd you end up going there that evening?"

Solomon again, "Please, Tina, let's bounce."

Harman waved off her attorney.

"Johnny called me at home just as I was sitting down to dinner…Blue Apron shrimp and stir-fry, it was excellent…he wanted to talk. I could tell he'd been drinking. I live in a restored townhouse in Homestead. He suggested we meet at that old strip mall in Munhall. He seemed desperate, so I agreed."

GK cocked a brow, "But you ate your stir fry first?"

"Sorry, Johnny Lessen wasn't worth cold stir-fry, late in the evening. So, yeah, I ate first. When I got to the mall, he was sitting out front in that stupid car. The old parking lot was filled with people flying drones and hanging out, probably buying and smoking weed. Johnny suggested we drive around to the rear of the mall, back by the loading docks. I used to go to that mall as a kid. It's sad."

"What did Lessen want?"

"As I said, he was drunk. He said the station was not going to renew his contract. He said we'd both be out on our asses. He wanted us to go see KDKA-TV as a team, make a deal with them."

"What'd you say?"

"I said, 'Johnny, old buddy old pal, if they're finally dropping you then I'm getting promoted from Triple A up to The Show.' And about time. I did not need KDKA, and I did not need the losing hassle of a breach-of-contract lawsuit. Mark Solomon's good, but he ain't that good." Harman winked at her attorney.

Maria White smiled and asked, "What was Lessen's reaction to that."

Turning her head, Tina Harman smiled at Maria and chuckled.

"Sister, I bet you know what it's like when you bitch-slap one of the boys. Lessen went crazy. Called me every misogynistic slur he could remember. Invented a few new ones, I think. Called me a traitor, disloyal, arrogant, blah, blah, blah. Swore he'd get a deal someplace and kick my boney ass in the ratings. It was a five-star Johnny Lessen hissy-fit."

"What did you do or say?"

"I said something like 'Johnny why don't you go slide down a razor blade into a pool of alcohol. It's been awful working with you, etc.' I advised him to not drive, he was pretty faced, strongly suggested he sleep it off there. Wouldn't want to mangle that pretty car. Then I drove away and went back home."

GK Hardace looked at Harman. "Why didn't you come see us on your own and tell us this?"

"Detective, I'm in the dirt racket like you. I knew you'd come calling soon. Here we are. Johnny Lessen's dead. His method of exiting this veil of tears theoretically troubles polite society. But it was Johnny Lessen. My guess is you would have a harder time finding someone who gave a s..., who cared, that Lessen was murdered than finding the murderer. I didn't kill the bastard. I don't know who did. I don't care at all."

"Pretty harsh," Maria whistled.

"Whatever. He's dead. He's gone. Good riddance."

Hardace tried to give her his best 'hardass' look.

"Ms. Harman, you had motive and opportunity. We could arrest you on suspicion."

"Detective, you don't have dick." Harman winked at White.

"Please arrest me for murdering Johnny Lessen. It'll be a great way to kick off my new show. I know the DA. He hates cases that aren't slam dunks. He'll not prosecute with the flimsy case you have against me. But, hell, arrest away."

Maria White cleared her throat. "Thank you, Ms. Harman, for coming in today. We appreciate your candor. Gentlemen."

"My stock and trade." Tina Harman stood and left with her legal barracuda.

"Now, she's a piece of work. I predict that in about ten years, you'll be investigating her murder. That no one will give a rat's patoot about. I'll be retired so it won't be my problem."

Maria shrugged, "Maybe Lessen was just offed by some random gang-bangers selling weed at that old strip mall."

"Did Lessen have any money?"

"He wasn't poor. He'd a couple mil. Left his brother a hundred K and everything else he gave to his college, Towson University, in Baltimore. He left them all his papers, including the boxes of death threats. He hoped they'd endow a chair or something in their School of Journalism. He's listed on their noted alumnae page on their website. They liked him, even if no one else did."

"So, no motive there," sighed GK.

"Nope."

"Ah, hell, sometimes I hate this job. Let's work on a case we can clear. Usually, when a celebrity gets iced, the mayor and everyone else is on our ass. This guy was so miserable, no one gives a hoot if we nail someone for it or not."

Chapter Four: Cold Case

The Lessen case went cold. And stayed cold. Hardace and White chased some random tips but they were BS. Just the usual jokers who like pulling cops' chains. Pittsburgh streets could be mean. The Detectives were kept busy chasing bad boys and girls. Lessen's folder just moved further back in their active file until it tumbled down to the cold drawer.

Six months after Lessen was murdered, Maria White drove out to Sewickley dogging a murder suspect being held there on child endangerment charges. The guy was a moron but had a solid alibi for White's case. She never liked him for it anyway.

White stopped in the station's canteen for a cup of bad coffee. Three suit guys invited her to join them. They were amused that her partner was GK Hardace.

"Old Hardass. How's that grump doing?"

White smiled. "If you know him, you know him."

"He's a legend. Made his bones closing a mass murder case about twenty-five years ago. Tell him, we just cleared a mass murder case out here in the subs."

The other cops laughed at that.

"Yep, we finally caught up with the Ted Bundy of autocide."

Maria shrugged. "What are you clowns talking about."

"Tell her, Mike. Tell the homicide detective how real cops stop the slaughter of innocents." More laughter.

A burly fellow in a tight sportscoat grinned.

"So, Maria, for the past three years, more or less, some goofball has been shooting up cars. From the airport all the way up to Beaver Falls, this nut has been taking a bump-stocked AR-15 and shooting the crap out of parked cars. Just for the hell of it. "

"That's crazy." Maria grinned.

"What's really crazy is that he only lit up Italian cars."

"Italian cars?" Mar laughed, but these boys had her interest. Big time.

"Yeah, Lamborghinis, Massarottis, Ferraris, Alfa-Romeos, Fiats, a couple of old Lancias. If it was an Italian car, this nut Harshman was killing it. We finally got a good security camera shot of the guy. A railroad guy from Munhall. He's locked up. Judge denied bail."

"Do you have ballistic info on this guy's gun?"

"He has three AR-15s. And, yeah, we have buckets of bullets. Shells too. Guy kept everything. Every bullet that we pulled out of one of those dead Italian cars came from his rifles. We got him, no doubt. Why?"

"I'm thinking about something," Maria said calmly. "He tell you why he did it?"

"Yeah. He confessed. Said his girlfriend ran off with some guy who drove an Italian sports car. He doesn't know which make or model. So, he just started blasting at any of them. Mostly in the western suburbs cause he thinks that's where this girl stealer lives.

He's whacko. We'll get to clear dozens of PD cases when he goes away."

"Anything else hinky about him?"

"That's not enough...Well he seems to like piloting drones too. We found two high end rigs in his truck. Probably spying on sunbathing coeds over at Duquesne."

Maria was all business now. "You guys remember Johnny Lessen?"

Mike lost his smile.

"I do. That guy ruined my ex-brother-in-law. Accused him of ripping off elderly folks with his plumbing business. He lost his business, started drinking, started whoring around, Began thumping my sister and the kids. She finally left him. I blame it all on that prick Lessen."

"You know we have never been able to close the Lessen murder case…"

"Who cares?"

"I think you might have Lessen's murderer in a cell down the hall."

Maria briefly told them about the Alfa and the old Munhall strip mall used by local droners.

"You think? Why would our guy want to shoot Lessen any more than four million other Lessen-haters?"

"Frankly, I don't think he intended to kill Johnny Lessen. I think your guy happened to be flying his drone one evening. He lives right there. Went behind the mall to take a leak and saw a parked Alfa-Romeo, apparently empty. Lessen was drunk and slumping down."

Maria finished her coffee and shrugged.

"This guy Harshman got in his truck, drove around back, and sprayed the Alfa, killing it and the lovable Johnny Lessen inside."

There was whistling all around among the coffee drinkers. Looks like the Sewickley PD might have solved the most high-profile murder in Pittsburgh in years.

Maria stood up and thanked the officers.

"Please send samples of each of the bullets and casings from his three guns to PPDHQ, to me, and we'll match them against the ones we dug out of Lessen and his poor car. Also, if his truck or phone are GPS enabled, those records might be useful too."

The Sewickley cops all stood and shook Maria's hand. She smiled.

"Thanks fellas, you have made my day."

Maria returned to her car. She called GK and gave him an update.

"I'll be damned. All this time we've been looking at the wrong murder victim."

Epilog

Ron Harshman confessed to assassinating an Alfa-Romeo, one night the previous summer, behind the Henry Street strip mall in Munhall. He hadn't paid any attention to the Lassen murder. He didn't follow anything but sports. He didn't know Lassen, didn't care a twig about him.

Harshman was sentence to twenty-eight to thirty-four and half years in state prison for the first-degree murder of more than two dozen Italian automobiles, and the second-degree murder of the cuddly Johnny Lessen.

Tina Harman's show "Hard Harman" was cancelled after three months due to ratings even more awful than Johnny Lessen's. She publicly blamed the sexist, ignorant citizenry of Pittsburgh. Her next job was as a part-time weekend anchor for WDUR-TV in Durango, Colorado.

Maria White was promoted to Detective First Class. GK was also promoted to Detective First Class. As he had done many times in the past, he turned down the promotion, even though that meant Maria became his boss.

"I like being a Detective. Besides, Maria, we both know who the real boss is around here."

Ghosts of the Bloody Lane

Notable Author: Edgar Allen Poe

Genre: Horror

Prompt: Using only 100 words place a character in an eerie or frightening atmosphere at night on the bleakest, foulest day of the year.

Prompt Forward

"I hate night duty."

U.S. Park Ranger Sarah Grice gazed out the Antietam National Battlefield headquarters' window. A glow flickered through the fog, like a campfire, down toward the Sunken Road.

"The hell?"

Ranger Grice slickered against the November night and started trudging toward the glow. Too foggy and miserable for the three-wheeler. As she neared the mounded ridge of Bloody Lane, Sarah heard tin plates clattering and neighing horses. And voices.

"We gave those blue Yankee dogs all they wanted this day."

A chuckle. "We did that. Those curs'll be back tomorrow."

Sarah shivered, and it wasn't just the November chill. Her heart trembled, and the hair on her nape stood stiff.

Chapter 1: Kin

Sarah inched toward the crest of the mound. The voices were distinct now.

"Shush, shush. I hear something out there."

"Oh, hell, Grice there ain't been nothing out there in a snake's age. It's just the wind."

Sarah thought, "Grice?" Her boot snapped a small branch. The voices stopped. The plates stopped clattering. Even the horses stopped neighing.

Sarah was tempted to crawl over the ridge and see what was going on. But the ground was muddy. She'd already muddied her boots and she didn't want to scrub her uniform pants.

"Besides," she thought, "I'm the damn authority around here."

She popped up tall and proud on the ridge crest, all five foot four of her and wearing her best cop face, one hand on her unsnapped holster.

Stretching in both directions along the Sunken Road was an endless row of scruffy, bearded men holding plates of food. Leaning against both banks of the road were dirty muskets, with bayonets affixed. Horses, and crude fires and torches and muddy satchels were scattered among the men. As were the occasional Confederate battle flag.

The men, Sarah assumed they were some kind of wannabe army, gaped open-mouthed at her. She snapped her holster. How did all these nutty re-enactors get down here unseen.

"What the hell are you jackasses up to? Where are your vehicles? Where's your friggin permit?"

She noticed most were dressed in just shirts and light tunics.

"And aren't you all freezing off your asses in this crap?" She waved her arms toward the bleak, foul night.

One of the assembled spoke.

"It sure looks like a gal tucked under that little brown uniform. But, by golly, that's some salty man words coming out of that pretty face." A ripple of laughter moved through the men.

"I'll give you bastards some salty man talk. I want to see who passes for the leader of you fools, and I want to see some righteous paperwork, and I want to see both now."

"Missy, it don't work like that." One of the men, indistinguishable from the others, came forward carrying a trench ladder.

"Why don't you come on down here and chew some fat with us. You'll be fine. No harms going to come your way, even though none of has seen a gal, especially a pretty gal, in a long time."

Sarah unsnapped her holster again.

"You can bet your mangy ass no harm's coming my way. I give the orders here. You try anything with me, every uniformed Federal hardass within a hundred miles of here will be on you monkeys like ugly on an ape."

That really caused a mirthic chuckle to ripple through the men.

"Darlin, you don't think we ain't well acquainted with Federal hardasses. I ain't never heard that word for those bastards, but I like it."

He leaned the ladder against the road bank and waved for Sarah to climb down. "Please, Missy."

"This is crazy," she thought, "this is stupid."

The ragtag re-enactor holding the ladder was not menacing, indeed he was almost reassuring. She climbed down the ladder, pretty much assuming these lugs were staring at her behind. They had gone back to their chow and were paying her no heed.

"Maybe, I need to get back to the gym," Sarah chuckled to herself.

"Be careful, now, missy. Sit here with this ol dead fellow and let's chat." He put two small, crude, wooden folding-benches against the road bank. "Take a load off."

"So, what do you mean 'ol dead fellow?'"

"You ain't figured it out yet? I'm dead. Kaput. We all are. Even the horses. Dead as doornails."

Sarah looked at the crazy old re-enactor.

"I think you may be getting into character a bit much. How'd you guys get here?"

"We are always here. Every day we fight and die and every night we wait to be hauled away."

Sarah was about to call the man "Old-timer," but she noticed that he really wasn't that old. Maybe not even older than her.

"What's your name? Are you the leader of these crackpots?"

"Nah. I'm just a dirt infantryman like most of these boys. We have some officers in our unlucky corps. But they get hauled away first and are all gone now. You need to come back earlier in the evening if you want to meet the brass."

"What in hell are you talking about?"

"It's just how it works around here. You notice how there are fewer fellows here now than when you first poked your pretty face over that hill?"

Sarah looked down in each direction. He was right. Surely looked like there were fewer re-enactors than before. Were they sneaking away? As she was staring, a scruffy young man, boy really, standing directly in front of her disappeared. In a blink, he was standing there then, gone. "What the…?"

"I'm going to be puffing away too, soon. And once I'm gone, I'm thinking you won't be seeing the rest of these…what'd you call us…jackasses anymore tonight."

The crowd was thinning. She turned to the man speaking to her, "Who are you?"

"My name's Jonathan Lacy Grice. Surprised? What's your name, gal?"

A church in distant Sharpsburg began pealing nine chimes.

"We better hurry, missy. I'll be disappearing soon.'"

"My name's Sarah Grice. What is going on, Jonathan?"

Sarah had lost all her bravado. She was genuinely overwhelmed, frightened. If this was real. If she wasn't dreaming or hallucinating somehow, she would be beyond confused, beyond measure.

"In a teapot, Sarah, I am one of your ancestors, maybe your great- great- great -grandpappy. I left a widow and three young boys back Stafford County. I was an infantryman in General Hill's corps posted here on the sunken road to hold the line and let our boys regroup to the south. We had us a fierce battle for hours with those blue devils. Somewhere in that hubbub, I was killed. Dead."

"You don't look dead to me Jonathan."

Sarah grabbed his hand, then dropped it. Jonathan's hand was as cold as steel inside the cryogenic chests Sarah had experienced in her engineering days.

"I'm dead. I'll be back here tomorrow to go through that hellish day all over. Then bivouac here till the grave patrols come and fetch me."

"I don't understand," whispered Sarah.

"We're here every day. This is our eternal punishment for our sins. We're ghosts. Sometimes, folks will catch glimpses of us. Or think they do. The only ones who can see us, talk to us, are our direct kin. Family. Like you. And only at night when we're waiting to be hauled away."

"How often does that happen?"

"In the early days, all the dang time. We'd see folks. Most of 'em ran like the dickens. I would have too if I'd been them. Nowadays, no one. You're the first in I don't know how long. Time ain't a big something here. I don't think folks are allowed around here at night. You been here before?"

"This is my first day of duty at Antietam. I was posted at Assateague. Jonathan…how do I explain you?"

Sarah noticed the number of ghostly soldiers was greatly reduced. As she turned back to look at Jonathan, he gave a small smile, and blinked out of sight. Then they all did, and the fires and torches and Sarah was plunged back into the freezing, miserable dark November night.

Chapter 2: Sarah

Miss Sarah Grice grew up among the swells in the suburbs of Baltimore County. Her parents broke up when she was six, leaving her and her younger brother to be raised primarily by her dad and his sprawling family, her aunts, and uncles.

The Grices are engineers, had been for generations. From an early age, Sarah, unsurprisingly, demonstrated a high aptitude for math and the sciences. She attended an all-girls' prep school, sweeping the STEP awards. Then into the University of Maryland engineering program, Cornel graduate school, advanced studies at the University of Tokyo.

Her proud family applauded her. They talked of the astronaut program. Or joining the family's 120-year-old consulting and construction firm. Maybe a PhD, then teaching engineering at a prestigious Ivy League university.

Upon her return from Tokyo, Sarah announced that she had enrolled in and been accepted to the Temple University Park Ranger Law Enforcement Academy. Oh, and she "hated, loathed engineering."

She excelled at the Academy and received an immediate full-time appointment to the Assateague Island National Seashore. After six years she received an appointment to the Antietam National Battlefield. Where, on her first night on the job, she ran into her great -great- great -grandpappy.

Sarah lived in Hagerstown with her long-term fiancé, a bullet-headed lump of muscle named Tim Hanna. Tim had been a corrections officer at the Maryland Eastern Correctional Institution and had easily transferred to the State's Hagerstown prison. He was crazy about Sarah. She was the one who preferred the long-term engagement.

After finding herself sitting in the wet dirt of the sunken road, in the dark, Sarah trudged back to the park's headquarters. She spent the rest of her shift reading on the battle and, especially, the fighting on Bloody Lane. Over 5,500 men were killed or wounded during the four hours of fighting along the lane. The battle was a draw. The exhausted armies then spent the rest of the day and night tending to their wounded and taking the dead away for burial.

Over the years, there had been many ghost sightings at the battlefield, especially around the Bloody Lane. In recent years, ghost stories became less told, probably because the Battlefield was closed at night and Rangers strictly enforced that policy.

When Sarah returned home, Tim was still working third trick at the prison. She had, by then, convinced herself that the evening was some kind of wild hallucination. Maybe she had a brain tumor. But her uniform was filthy. She went to bed and joined Tim on their enclosed deck for brunch around noon the next day.

"Tim, you know anything about the Battle of Antietam?"

"I know my family in Georgia call it the Battle of Sharpsburg. Other than that, I know Lee tried to invade the North, got stopped at Antietam and had to hustle back to Virginia. A ton of soldiers were killed there. Those guys loved slaughtering one another. Gettysburg, Shiloh, Vicksburg…nothing civil about that Civil War."

"It must have been terrible to be a soldier back then," Sarah muttered.

"Well, I guess it was worth it at Antietam. Even though the battle was pretty much a tie, Lincoln declared it a victory, then signed the Emancipation Proclamation a few days later."

Sarah punched Tim's arm." Look at you, Mr. Civil War historian. How do you know so much?"

"Well, it's funny you should be asking those things. Though, if you're going to work there you should know stuff."

"I'm only pulling night duty now. Eventually, I'll get my tour certification and be able to show folks around and answer questions. Got a lot of holes in the education right now."

"I said, 'it was funny you asking.' I was watching an old *Finding Your Family* on YouTube yesterday…you know the PBS show about people's roots and ancestors…and that guy Jonah Elias Yates who hosts the show mentioned Antietam."

"Oh, yeah, what'd he say?"

"He's Black, you know, and he was saying one of his long-ago ancestors…a white dude…fought for the Rebs and was killed at Antietam. Yates grew up right down the road in Hancock."

"That's ironic. He tells many of his guests that they had slave owners or Confederates in their family way back when. Most of them don't know that, and don't particularly like to find out. And Jonah Elias Yates has some in his family bible too. Funny."

"Well, you can't pick your relatives, and you sure can't pick your ancestors. Our families are both from Maryland, been here a long time, we might have some slavers back there too."

"I hope not. I think the Grices originally came from Virginia."

"Ha," laughed Tim, "that's worse."

"You have no idea," thought Sarah. She decided not to tell Tim about last night. He'd think she was nuts or want her to get an MRI. Piss on it. She finished her brunch and headed to the laundry room to hand scrub her uniform.

Chapter 3: Second Night

Sarah's shift didn't start until 8:00 pm officially, but she went in an hour early yesterday and today she showed up at 6:30. The unit commander, Sargent Judy Brouse, was in the office.

"Hey, Grice, coming in early. Seems like you're brownnosing me. I like that in a Ranger."

"Hey, Sargent, I'm just trying to get my sea legs. Spent the last six years chasing incontinent ponies all over Assateague. Not sure what kind of trouble to look out for here."

"Horny teenagers, mostly. Some poachers. Asshats who spray paint the monuments or steal memorials. I did the incontinent ponies tour myself back in the 90s. Got a nice tan."

"I was reading on the battle last night."

"Good girl."

"I read a couple places about ghosts and hauntings. Anything hinky ever go on?"

"Well, I'll tell you something, Grice. This is the spookiest place on earth. It's ungodly quiet day and night. You feel presences, but in twenty-five years, I've never seen a Casper. If you spot one, tell him for me that all those poor bastards were friggin nuts to be killing and butchering each other. They were all Americans, for godssake."

"I'll tell 'em, Ma'am, if I see one."

"You do that Grice. Since you're here, I'll go home to my lazy husband, sitting lazy in his Lazy Boy. But I love the sonovabitch."

"Good evening, Sargent."

The clocks had already fallen back, so darkness engulfed the Battlefield at seven o'clock. The November night was bitter. The skies cleared and a full moon shown big and bright. Sarah peered through the window towards the Bloody Lane She could detect no flickering campfires in the bright moonlight. Even with binoculars.

"Ah, the hell with it."

Sarah donned her heavy coat and headed towards the lane. She again forsook the three-wheeler, this time out of a fear of spooking the …spooks. As she neared the mound of the road bank, Sarah thought she did see lights flickering. Then she heard the clattering of mess plates and horses and then, a familiar voice.

"Hush, fellas, I believe my great-great-great-grandbaby is coming to visit us again. Ain't that dandy? Where' my ladder?"

When Sarah crested the mound, she saw an even larger throng of scruffy Confederate soldiers milling along the length of the sunken road. She thought, "I guess the grave boys haven't gotten here yet tonight."

Jonathan leaned the trench ladder against the road bank and Sarah climbed down, not worrying this time about butt ogling re-enactors.

"Evening Sarah"

"Jonathan. Just checking back to make sure I wasn't having delirium last night."

"It's nice to see you again, darlin."

Jonathan again produced the two benches. The rest of the ghosts let them be.

"Can those other guys see and hear me too? Can they talk to me?"

"Sure, they can. But they won't unless you ask them directly. You're my kin. My guest. They know that and they respect that."

"And you'll be here every night. If I brought my fiancé, would he see you too?"

"Probably not. Only if he has kin here too. And if he can't see us, you won't see us either. They're the dad-gum rules here."

"But you'll be here every night?"

"Every night. Every damn night. And every damn day, killing and dying all over again. In the morning, at dawn, we go back to being who we were in 1862. All hepped up to fight. Kill them Yankee curs. We end up being the killed bastards. Then at sunset, we become who we are now. We eat grub even though we know we don't need it. We talk about things. Back in the old days, fellas would try to go over the top, or stick a bayonet in their own bellies. Next day, they're right back here. "

Sarah shook her head and touched Jonathan's shoulder. He was bony and his light clothing did little to keep the deep coldness of his being from her fingers.

"I'm sorry, Jonathan. Do you have any idea what's going on in the living world."

"A little. When we got visitors back right after the war, we heard that we lost the war, Lincoln got shot and the slaves got freed which caused all kind of trouble back home."

"Did you own slaves, Jonathan?"

"Oh. Hell, no. We didn't need them. Didn't want them. Slavery was a terrible thing to do to folks. Most of these fellas never owned a slave. We fought this war, we did, to protect our States. We weren't fighting to protect slavery. And the ones what did, now know they were wrong in doing so. Bad wrong."

Sarah smiled and thought, "There you go, Jonah Elias Yates. My Virginia kin might have fought for the Confederacy, but they didn't own slaves, thank God."

Thinking about the PBS host made Sarah remember her conversation with Tim.

"Here's another question for you Jonathan, is there anyone named Yates among these ghos…fellas?"

Jonathan grinned through his unkempt beard. "We're ghosts, we know it. We don't like it. And yep, there are several Yates here and about on this cursed lane."

"Were any of the Yates slave holders?"

"Probably the only was Captain Yates. He had a big farm up around Winchester, so I'm sure he had slaves. Why?"

"Just curious. Could I speak to him? Would he speak with me?"

"How long have we been here, Sarah?"

"Over 160 years."

"Damn. Been that long? Gates hasn't spoken to no darn body but us old horse turds in probably 160 years. I'm sure he'd love to chat. You're easy on the eyes too, so he'll probably trip on his sword running over here. I'll go fetch the captain."

Captain Thomas Dewey Yates was a kid. He might have been born 185 years ago, but he looked no more than 25. He had some wispy facial hair, long flowing blonde locks, and an officer's uniform much crisper than the infantrymen like Jonathan.

"Ma'am, pleasure meeting you. I heard you barking orders at these sorry 'jackasses' last night. You could have gone to West Point with that kind of grit and command."

"I thought about it, Family had the appointment all lined up but it wasn't for me."

Captain Yates' smile turned into a look of confusion. He looked at Jonathan for help.

Sarah grinned. "Sorry Captain. They let women into West Point now."

"Ain't that something?"

"Captain, do you mind if I ask you some questions about your farm up near Winchester?"

"Not at all."

"I assume you owned slaves. We're any of them blood relatives of yours?"

"Well, Ma'am, you don't beat around the lilac bush, do you? I am now so ashamed of my slave owning ways that you cannot embarrass me with your straightforward ways. I only know of one slave who was probably kin. Eli. Eli and I were about the same age. We were great friends as children. We ran all over tarnation up in those hills. Eli had a momma who was pretty and worked in our house after my momma died birthing my brother Joseph."

"I'm sorry Captain."

"Thank you, Ma'am, that's kind of you."

Yates tapped his cap and continued.

"Eli never knew who was his daddy. His momma wouldn't say. But Eli thought my daddy was his daddy. I did too. We thought we were brothers but as Eli grew big and older, he had to go work in the fields. My daddy never gave him no slack. When my daddy died in '58, the first thing I did when I inherited the farm was set Eli and his momma free. I gave them two horses and some money, and they left to start a new life up in Maryland somewhere."

"That was noble of you Captain."

"I kept all the other slaves. No, I was as bad as my daddy. Maybe worse seein as how I knew better. Eli was one of my brothers. Any of those slaves could have been my brother, or sister. I was a bad man and I'll suffer here on this miserable sunken road for eternity for my wickedness. And deservedly so. Night, Ma'am."

Sarah watched Captain Yates walk again through the thinning ranks. He had no sword to trip over. Then he just blinked away. She turned back to Jonathan who had said nothing during her talk with Yates.

"That's curious," said Jonathan, "the grave boys usually pluck the officers first but they let the captain stick around to chat with you. They steal me away when we're talking. Damn officers get privilege, even in Hades."

"Jonathan, is there no release for you from this Groundhog Day hell?"

"Groundhog Day, what is that?"

"Forget it, are you stuck here for eternity?"

"I'm ascared we are. The Bible thumpers here…and there are many…believe the only way we can make this stop is to be forgiven for the original sin of slavery. And the only one who can do that is a slave. "

"How's that going to happen?"

"It ain't, that's the problem. Some kin of someone here, who was a slave, would have to come here, like you have, and hear our confessions, our apologies and grant us absolution. That's what the Bible boys say, and we got no better answer."

The Sharpsburg church bell had rung nine times while Sarah was talking to Captain Yates.

"I'm going to be fetched soon Sarah. Thank you for coming again tonight." And with that he blinked away, and the Bloody Lane turned dark and empty again.

Chapter 4: Jonah Elias Yates

Getting back home to Hancock was always a pain. There was no scheduled air service. A passenger train barreled through once a day but didn't stop. The only way to get there reasonably was to fly privately into Hagerstown, then bum a ride the 30 miles to Hancock, and repeat the process to get the devil back.

Dr. Jonah Elias Yates… brightest star in the Harvard faculty, world renown scholar, friend of presidents, media darling…was returning to his hometown of Hancock because he had promised his dying mother last year that he would give the eulogy for his half- brother (half-wit brother) Carlton who was also dying. Today was that day.

Yates arranged a private jet, through an admirer, to fly back and forth to Hagerstown. He phoned his good friend the Secretary of the Interior to see if he could arrange round-trip car service between the Hagerstown Airport and Hancock. The Secretary made that happen.

Yates landed in Hagerstown, made his way through the modest terminal, and spied a fetching young woman in a Park Service uniform waiting beside a Park Service Ford. Not a town car but he could slum it one time. For his mother.

"Let me help you Dr. Yates, with your bag."

"Thank you, young lady. How long to Hancock?"

"It's clear sailing. Thirty minutes."

The eulogy went fine. Carlton wasn't such a bad guy. He loved their mother and took care of her until she finally agreed to move to Boston with Jonah. Because of the late hour of the service, Yates was spending the night at the Airport Inn. The private jet would pick him up at 8:00 am the following morning.

Yates felt good. His eulogy was quite Yatesian in its humor and wisdom and gratitude towards Carlton. He'd seen a few old pals he hadn't seen since leaving Hancock. He felt like chatting.

"Young lady, how long have you been with the Park Service?"

"Almost ten years, sir."

"So, what kind of education do you have that got you that job? An AA, maybe?"

"I have a degree in Advanced Metal Engineering from University of Maryland, a master's degree in Space Engineering from Cornel, and did post-graduate studies in rocketry and AI at the University of Tokyo. I also have 900 hours of course work in Park Rangering from Temple."

Yates smiled a genuine smile.

"Well, now, don't I feel like a horse's ass. You are utterly fascinating. Can we have dinner this evening?"

"I have a boyfriend…fiancé…who has a head as big as that car hood and weighs 230 pounds with about 8% bodyfat. He's a guard at a max pen."

"Oh, dear. You never fail to impress. Miss, Miss, …?"

"Sarah Grice."

"Miss Sarah Grice. Sorry for the condescending jackassery. I'll try not to bother you anymore."

"No worries, Doctor. Do you mind if I ask you some questions? Kind of "Find Your Family" questions."

"Sure."

"Does the name Captain Thomas Dewey Yates ring a bell?"

The good Doctor, who was sitting in the backseat, stared into the side window, then turned and spoke again to Sarah.

"That name rings many bells. Some good, mostly bad. How do you know that name?"

"How about Eli Yates? That one ring better bells?"

"Stop the car Sarah, I need to move to the front seat so we can better chat."

She pulled over on Interstate 70 and he hopped into the front seat.

"So, Sarah, did you read my biography? Is that how you know about Thomas Yates and Eli Yates?"

"I did read your book. Fascinating. Rags to riches. Hancock to Harvard. You've had a terrific life. My fiancé is a big fan of your show."

"The muscle-bound prison guard? Not you? You don't like my show?"

"Oh, it's fine."

Yates cocked an eyebrow, "But?"

"I think sometimes you go after some of your white guests a little much. If somewhere in their murky gene pool, they had a slave owning ancestor. You seem to want them to be mortified and apologetic about long dead relatives that have no bearing on their current lives."

Yates smiled.

"Couple things. You're hardly the first to point that out. Second, my guests are super-privileged celebrities who can use a little mortification. It's good TV. It's my brand."

"Do you believe that descendants of slave-owners are genetically inclined to be, say, more flawed, more racist maybe, than people whose ancestors weren't slavers?" Sarah smiled.

"You are a curiosity Sarah, I must say. I probably do think the apple doesn't fall far from the great-great-great-grandtree."

Sarah turned her head quickly towards Yates.

"You're descendent from a multi-generational family of slaveholders. That make you flawed, racist?"

"Touché. Again, something that has not not been pointed out before. I blame all my bad points...and they are legend...on those terrible slave-owning ancestorial scum."

"I work at Antietam. You know one of your slaveholding ancestors died there?"

"Yeah, irony is a bitch."

"Captain Thomas Dewey Yates, III. I've gotten to know him well over the past four years. Would you like to make his acquaintance?"

Yates snorted and tapped his head.

"What is he some chubby, local re-enactor? They're a dying breed."

"Nope, he's the real deal. Your 185-year-old cousin. Let me tell you a story you are not going to believe."

Sarah drove thirty miles recapping her past four years among the ghosts of Bloody Lane. Dr. Yates sat silent.

"So, Doc, what do you say? Wanna take a trip to the Twilight Zone? I went to much trouble to arrange being your driver today just to get you to take a stroll down Bloody Lane with me. You won't regret it."

"Damn girl, you're crazy. It's already dusk. You want me to go down to that battlefield with you now, traipse around in the dark looking for Confederate ghosts?"

Sarah chuckled. "You got it, Doc. Game?"

"I usually have some security with me. You're supposed to be my security today. And you want to kidnap me."

"I thought about kidnapping you. But I think you're intellectually curious enough, authentic enough to at least check out where your long-dead relative died defending something you hate to your core. At night just makes it more dramatic. And I can tell you like the drama."

Jonah Elias Yates took a long gaze at Sarah Grice's intelligent, pretty face.

"I'm looking at a lonely dinner at a hotel restaurant. Piss on that. Let's do it, baby, let's go ghost hunting."

Chapter 5: Absolution

Sarah and Dr. Yates arrived at the Battlefield headquarters parking lot about 7:15 pm on a March evening. Sarah checked in with Ranger Eddie Holland, who had recently transferred to this posting and like all newbies was pulling the night shift. Sarah was now a day Ranger and a fully certified tour leader.

"Hey, Eddie, my buddy Jonah and I are going to take a little stroll around the park."

"You're good Sarah. Enjoy. Not too chilly out there tonight."

Sarah led Dr. Yates down the path towards the sunken road.

"Damn, Sarah, this place is spooky. Hard to believe all those thousands of soldiers dying here in a day or two. Humanity is just crazy sometimes."

As they neared the mound, Sarah saw the flickering light from the campfires and lanterns.

"You see that, Doc?"

"I hope this is some elaborate punk ruse. Cause I'm getting shaky."

"You'll get shakier."

They both heard clattering dishes and horses and, finally, voices.

"I think Sarah's coming for a visit. That's nice. What's the matter Captain? You sense something too?"

"I do, Jonathan, I do."

Sarah took Dr. Gates by his hand and helped him climb to the ridge top. When they got to the crest, they stood tall and gazed out onto the ragtag faces of General Hill's slaughtered brigade, milling in the sunken road.

Dr. Yates whispered to Sarah.

"This is unbelievable. My reality is forever shaken. Thank you for bringing me here."

All the soldiers stared at Dr. Gates. He sensed no sinister overhang, no animosity, no anger. He felt completely comfortable. A young officer stepped to the foreground and looked up at Jonah Elias Yates who, in turn, looked down and nodded in recognition. The officer smiled, snapped a sharp salute, and then began to applaud.

Like a match thrown on a vast field of dry underbrush, the ghosts of Bloody Lane followed Captain Yates' example, came to attention, saluted smartly, and applauded. The applause moved up and down the lane.

Jonah, misty eyed, turned to Sarah. "I don't know what to say."

"Would you like to go down and meet your cousin and the other soldiers?"

"Yes, I very much would." Sarah waved to Jonathan to bring the trench ladder.

Sarah and Dr. Yates climbed down and were greeted by Jonathan and Captain Yates. Sarah advised Dr. Yates not to make physical contact with the dead Confederates. They'd understand.

Captain Yates stepped forward, nodded to his cousin, and laughed.

"If your name ain't Eli, it should be. You're his dead ringer, with a few years added."

"My middle name is Elias. In my great-great-great grandfather Eli's diary, he wrote that Thomas Dewey Yates the third was his brother and the best friend he ever had. He heard that you had been killed at Appa…here…and he was heartbroken."

"He was my brother. My friend. How we treated Eli and his mother and how the whole South treated slaves was shameful and sinful. We here on the lane know that now. It took getting killed and 160 years of talking about it here in our eternal hell. We deserve our eternal damnation. "

"Thank you, Captain." Dr Gates was clearly moved.

Then Jonathan spoke, "We don't ask your forgiveness. We are beyond forgiveness. What we all was a part of was evil and disgraceful. We wish the descendants of slaves to find much joy in their lives. We want what we done to never be forgotten so others don't fall into the terrible devilry we done."

Dr. Yates nodded.

"Slavery was evil. Humans can be unbelievably cruel to one another." He shook his head.

Sarah gestured towards the other soldiers.

"Doctor, why don't we take a little walk down the Sunken Road. You can meet some of the boys before the grave diggers take them away tonight."

As they walked among the ghosts, ghost soldiers saluted Dr. Graves and told him in all the dialects of the southern states how they were wrong and sorry.

Suddenly, Dr. Gates exclaimed, "They're all gone. Everything, gone."

Sarah had told him that once Captain Yates disappeared, Jonah would probably lose contact.

"We should go now."

She handed Dr. Yates her flashlight and they walked up the lane to the ladder. Sarah had heard the church bells and knew Jonathan would be blinking away soon also.

As they reached the ladder, Sarah said to Jonathan, "I'll come see you soon, Ol' Pappy."

"Don't you be worrying about us old dead guys. You live your life. And thank Mr. Yates. The boys feel a whole lot better seeing and meeting the fine gentleman."

Sarah passed Jonathan's message to Dr. Gates who spoke into the darkness in the general direction of Jonathan.

"Mr. Grice, you tell that cousin of mine, I'm coming back soon to interview him and you and many others. I'm going to write a book. A movie. No one will believe me but I'm going to do it. I love these fellas. I never thought I'd say that about Confederate soldiers."

Sarah announced that she was now also in the dark, that Jonathan had disappeared. As she had before when left in the darkness, she and Dr. Yates walked up the lane, then back to her car.

As Sarah drove the short distance to Hagerstown, Dr. Yates tried to contain his excitement over the night's events.

"Thank you, Sarah, for a most amazing experience. I don't know how you arranged to be my driver today. You are obviously brilliant and ungodly capable. Please come work for me."

"Thanks, Doctor. I'm doing what I'm supposed to be doing. You have a nice flight tomorrow."

"We'll be seeing more of each other, young lady. I must be in Boston for several days, but I'll be back here soon. I'm not kidding about that book. I guess our friends have been out there 160 plus years, a few days won't matter to them."

"Probably right, sir. Take care."

"Good night, Sara. Say hello to your big lug for me."

Epilogue

The next evening Sarah returned to the Bloody Lane. She waited well into the evening's darkness. General Hill's army of Confederate ghosts did not appear. Sarah was not surprised or saddened. She would like to have said farewell to Jonathan. It was time for him and the others to move on.

Dr. Yates was also not surprised when Sarah called to let him know the ghosts of Blood Lane had, at last, moved on to the next waystation of their journey.

"Simply recognizing the error of their ways in that fraught Purgatory was not enough. They had to also express the sincerity of their sorrow and guilt to a descendant of a slave."

"You may be right, sir."

"Oh, you figured it all out a long time ago. You are a brilliant woman, Sarah Grice."

"Just a humble Park Ranger, Dr. Yates. Sorry about your book."

"Oh, trust me Sarah, there is still going to be a book. Did you know my old cousin Captain Thomas Dewey Yates had a younger brother, Joseph?"

"I did ."

"And that Joseph was killed in Pickett's Charge at Gettysburg? Guess where I'll be hanging out in the dark?"

"Wow, good luck with that."

"Sarah, one last question. Had you not convinced me to accompany you to Antietam, and you were not prepared to kidnap me, what would you have done?"

Sarah grinned into her phone.

"Oh, I had a Plan B, Jonah. I was going to take you back to your hotel and seduce you into impregnating me. Then, I'd have a slave descendant Yates all my own."

Jonah Elias Yates roared.

"By damn, woman, you are brilliant. Sorry I missed Plan B. Stay well, Sarah Grice."

Missing Linker

Notable Author: Benjamin Quarles (Feb 2019)

Genre: People's History
Prompt: Using up to 100 words, portray a character from an oppressed group acting as an agent of change during a critical wartime period or event.

Prompt Forward

Kiki stared at the sleeping airman.

"He looks like an angel…an angel who dropped from the sky," she thought.

She tucked the parachute tighter, a poor blanket for a stone barn in Brittany. He'd crashed through the straw roof last night. But heat was not really the problem; he was hot with fever. He moaned.

His flight jacked bore the name "Jimmy."

"Hush, my brave Angel Jimmy," she whispered, "The Boche are everywhere. We'll protect you and make you well and send you back to some lucky American girl."

She kissed his forehead and stood to go find her brother Jacques.

Chapter 1: Fersfield-Winfarthing Airbase

Twenty-four hours earlier...

Ensign James "Jimmy" Linker sipped bad coffee in the officers Quonset. He vaguely heard aircraft outside, motors revving, men shouting. Linker was lost in his own thoughts. He'd skipped Sunday chapel. He was angry, pissed and not good company. He'd remember August 13, 1944, the rest of his life.

Linker felt a large hand grip his shoulder. "Okay if I join you, Jimmy?"

Captain Mike Green smiled tersely at Ensign Linker.

"Certainly, sir. Sit down."

"Jimmy, I heard about Kennedy and Willy. I'm sorry. I knew you had been Joe's co-pilot for a while now. He was a good man, a good pilot."

Linker looked at Captain Green.

"I should have been on that plane. Lieutenant Willy pulled rank on me and jumped in my chair. Joe and I would have made it work."

"Willy was just doing his job. He was the Unit's Exec and felt it his place to go. You're sitting here now, crying in your coffee because he jumped in that seat."

"Joe and I would have got it done, sir. We kicked ass up there. Joe might have been a rich guy with everything going for him, but he was a great pilot. And I made him even better. Willy should have just let us go."

"Jimmy, it was most likely a random spark that blew up the plane, probably when Joe armed the Torpex. Willy had nothing to do with it. Joe and Willy, they got blown to pieces all over Suffolk because sometimes God is a prick."

"Yes, sir." Linker sipped his lousy coffee.

"The reason, I'm sitting here now Jimmy is to remind you that Joe's mission, this whole project, is still very hush hush. 'Aphrodite' is still a go. You're still assigned to Special Air Unit 1 and expected to keep your mouth shut. Mourn Joe but move on. Got it?"

"Yes, sir."

"Good, man. Now I need you to get back on the horse immediately. Tonight, you and Goeller will fly a bigshot Frenchie secretly into Brittany. Colonel Albert Eon. He's going to command a group of Resistance fighters in support of the Army's 8th and 20th Corps. They plan to run Jerry out of the U-boat pens in Brest, Lorient, and St. Nazaire."

"Yes, sir. Goeller's a fine pilot too."

"Alright, son. Goeller's prepping a Black Widow in Hangar H. He has mission specifics. Good luck. And, Jimmy, I am sorry about Joe."

"Thank you, sir. Me too. And Willy."

Captain Green squeezed Linker's shoulder again as he walked away.

Jimmy found Ensign Goeller walking around a not new, but not too beat up P-61.

"Hey, Guy"

"Jimmy-boy. Ready for a vacation in France?"

"Ready to go. What time we haulin?"

"1830."

"Okay. The cargo here?"

"He's back there in the hangar. Can't miss him. All nose and pomposity. Jimmy, sorry to hear about Joe."

"Thanks, Guy. See you later."

Colonel Albert Eon stood erect, dressed in crisp battle fatigues, talking to some enlisted men and seeming to genuinely enjoy their company. Maybe he wasn't so pompous after all.

Linker walked up to the Frenchman and saluted smartly.

"Colonel Eon, sir. I am Ensign James Linker. I will be co-piloting you this evening."

Eon returned the salute, then extended his hand.

"Good to meet you, Ensign. I hope we'll have an uneventful flight. Looking forward to getting home to France in one piece."

"Should be fine, sir. We'll be flying over the water most of the time, west of Normandy. Since D-Day, there is little Jerry activity in the air at night. The P-61 Black Widow is a fine night fighter. We should have you back in your homeland in a couple of hours."

"Excellent, Ensign. See you at 1830."

As advertised, the flight was uneventful. Colonel Eon sat in the gunner's chair while Goeller and Linker flew the plane. The weather was fine, the evening clear. But for the terrible war raging on the continent below, the flight could have been just a friendly jaunt on a summer's night off the coast of France.

The landing area was a crude field outside of Josselin. Goeller had flown into the area before, and Linker was not called upon to extend himself as a navigator. They came in high over the coast then dropped down to 2000 feet to fly into the interior.

Right on cue at 2045 hours, a pasture lit up with electric torches outlining a landing strip. Goeller brought the plane in for a bouncy landing, rolled to the end of the runway then spun the plane around.

Colonel Eon thanked Goeller and Linker. They wished him luck and he jumped down into a welcoming committee of Resistance fighters. Ensign Goeller immediately pushed the throttle and the Black Widow scurried down the makeshift runway and bounded into the August night. The landing lights went dark.

The takeoff was smooth and they quickly climbed to 5500 feet. The plane suddenly bounced like it hit a pothole.

"The hell?" Goeller calmly said into his intercom mic. "That was not flak, Linker. I know flak."

"Me too," agreed Linker, "a big ass bird?"

"Not this high up. I'm worried that either Mr. Pratt or Mr. Whitney left a monkey wrench in one of those engines."

The plane began to shake, and then shake more violently. A loud bang and a bright flickering in the window followed.

"Jesus Christ, Number One is on fire, Get out." Goeller's voice was no longer calm. "Now."

Linker could tell Goeller was fighting the plane and trying to hold it level for him to bail. He pulled his canopy back and climbed over the side opposite the burning engine. He flung himself into the night and hadn't fallen very far when the P-61 exploded.

Linker was struck by plane debris on his legs and shoulder and knocked unconscious by the explosion. He came to after some seconds, tumbling into the night. He wasn't sure if he was over land or water. He had no choice anyway. He pulled his ripcord.

His parachute had been torn by exploding plane debris, but opened and righted and slowed Linker's descent. He lost consciousness again, and fell unawares through the thatch roof of a small barn in Brittany, soon to be mistaken as an angel.

Chapter 2: Kiki

The next morning…

Kiki rose to go in search of her brother. She heard a loud motor noise draw up the lane and shut off, she guessed, in front of the farmhouse. She knew that was not Jacques. He had no such motorized beast.

Kiki spread straw over the unconscious airman, hiding him as best she could. She stepped from the hayloft and grimaced at the hole in the barn's roof. She started towards the barn door, hoping to sneak around and slide into the forest. A large figure filled the frame of the door, a fearsome silhouette, backlit by the morning light.

"Ah, Mademoiselle, you are just the person I seek."

He was a German soldier, huge and Aryan and besmocked in a grayish green uniform. He spoke rough but passable French. He was trouble and Kiki knew it.

"I'm sorry, sir, do I know you?"

"Alas, no. I have seen you in the village, hurrying to your chores. You are far too lovely to not notice. I have wanted to approach you. I know you are a war widow and I fear you do not appreciate the attention of your German liberators."

"You are right. What can I do for you this morning?"

She was praying that Jacques would not appear. Please, Jacques, stay away.

"I fear that I must be leaving Brittany soon. The Americans are pushing this way. We have been ordered to reinforce the port cities and abandon the interior. I will be heading east to defend the Fatherland. I am Karl, by the way." Karl shrugged his big shoulders.

"And what does any of that have to do with me?"

"Well, before I go, I wanted to have a little souvenir of France."

He stepped closer towards Kiki, "and you are the souvenir I have chosen."

Kiki slid against a stall. She could not run to the door. He blocked her escape and was probably as fit as an Olympic speed skater.

Karl came towards her.

"Ah, mon cherie, I think that you will enjoy your visit from Karl. That, like me, you will have fond memories of our time this morning."

"Keep away from me, you German swine."

"Oh my, German swine. Perhaps, this morning's memories will not be so pleasant for you after all."

With that, the swine stepped close to Kiki and was reaching out for her. A loud retort of a gunshot accompanied the shredding of the German's tunic high on his left arm. Karl flinched in pain and turned to see where the shot originated.

As he did so, Kiki grabbed a pitchfork that was leaning on the stall and drove all four tines deep into the German's belly. Olympic ice skater or not, Kiki's adrenalin rage buried the fork mortally within that swine's gut.

The German looked back at Kiki, the lust in his eyes turned to surprise and then to eternity. He dropped to the barn floor.

Kiki looked passed the late Karl and saw the American airman leaning on the stepdown from the hayloft, shakily holding his service Colt.

Angel Jimmy smiled at Kiki. His French was fine.

"I think that mort was not quite as petite as he hoped. Remind me to not make you angry."

Jimmy collapsed once more into unconsciousness.

Chapter 3: Jimmy

Ensign Jimmy Linker awoke in a straw stuffed, but surprisingly comfortable, bed in what was clearly a bedroom in an ancient farmhouse. Apprising him was the lovely girl he'd seen shish kabob that German bastard.

"Good afternoon, Jimmy Linker." She pronounced it Link-ay.

"Uh, good afternoon??"

"Kiki."

"Ah, good afternoon, Kiki. Sorry I wasn't much help earlier today."

"You were splendid. My hero. And that happen four days ago."

"Oh, dear."

"You were a very sick boy. Infections, I think. Very hot. We were afraid you might be joining Karl. But the fever said adieu and here you are."

"How did I get here?"

"My brother Jacques put you in a hand cart and we pushed you from the barn to here. We got you undressed and cleaned your bad wounds. Ouch. And got you into bed. Your parachute is buried with Karl in the woods. I cleaned your uniform as best I could."

"Whose sleeping clothes are these?"

'My brother's. My dead husband's. They are for you."

"How did I get into these clothes."

"I put them on you, of course."

"That's a little embarrassing."

"I have been a widow for over three years. So, naturally, I peeked."

"Well, then I owe you one."

"Be careful, flyboy, remember Karl."

"I don't think you have to worry. I feel pretty damn weak."

"You should eat. You have only sipped water for four days. I'll bring goat cheese and bread. See if you can handle that. We will make you a fat American again, Jimmy Link-ay."

The next morning, Linker was feeling stronger. He dressed in the clean clothes Kiki had placed on a chair and hobbled downstairs. He smelled eggs and bacon, and they smelled wonderful. Jacques looked up and smiled.

"Sit down Jimmy. Eat. Kiki is not only beautiful. She is also a marvelous cook."

"Shut up, Jacques."

Jimmy grinned, "Watch out, Jacques. I've seen what she can do with a fork."

Jacques' smiling face lost its smile and he said to Jimmy, "Kiki told me what you did. Merci, mon ami. I will always be indebted to you."

"Well, Kiki did all the heavy lifting. I shot his shirt sleeve."

Kiki sat down, "Enough you two. Eat Jimmy. Do you like fresh eggs?"

"Whenever we would be sent on a dangerous mission, we would get fresh eggs for breakfast. Otherwise, powdered eggs. The eggs were worth the danger."

"No dangerous missions today. After breakfast, you will walk with me through the forest to rebuild your strength. Every day we will walk further. If you don't keep up with me, no eggs for breakfast."

Each day, the routine was the same. Jimmy would eat breakfast with Jacques and Kiki. Then he and Kiki would take a brisk hike through the Brittanian forest that abutted their wheat and dairy farm. Jacques would go work the farm with his crew of local farmhands.

One morning, Jimmy asked Jacques, "These fellas have seen me around, are you not worried one might say something that the Germans would hear?"

Jacques shook his head.

"Non, these men are all in the Resistance. They hate the Germans. I am their squad leader. Worry not, mon ami."

"Okay, thanks. Is Jacques the French equivalent of Jack in my country?"

Jacques and Kiki both laughed.

"Jacques is how we say James. Jacques is a Jimmy too."

In the afternoons, after their walks, Kiki would attend to her many chores around the farm. Linker tried to make himself useful to Jacques. He had trained as a civil engineer before the war and was handy with machines.

Jacques and his crew were mighty impressed with the improvements Jimmy made to some of their ancient farm machinery. One of the men said, "We thought you Americans were just cowboys."

After dinners, Kiki, her brother, and Jimmy would sit outside in the late summer evenings, talk, and drink local wine. Jimmy learned that Kiki's husband had been killed at Dunkirk, fighting with the brave and doomed French and Belgium forces that kept the Germans at bay long enough for the evacuation to be successful. Their parents had died before the war and left the farm to them both. Jacques had never married, but he'd been seeing a village girl for years.

"You better be careful, Jacques," Kiki laughed one evening, "Some handsome American flyboy might fall through Marie's roof tonight and steal her away from you."

Jimmy grew stronger and fitter. He knew that soon, he should try to hook up with Allied troops. As Karl told Kiki, the local German patrols had fled back east, or been redeployed to the coastal cities where fighting was apparently brutal. Jacques knew from his Resistance connections that the American and organized Resistance combat units were not far away.

Jimmy would hate to go.

Chapter 4: Au Revoir

One day, Kiki did not make her usual breakfast. She was going to the village to do some shopping but would return in the early afternoon.

"We will do our walk then, Jimmy, the most strenuous one yet. And then we will have a picnic."

As promised, the afternoon walk was brisk and rugged. Kiki made Jimmy carry a heavy knapsack with their picnic lunch. They stopped at a small meadow overlooking an ancient granite quarry, filled now with water.

"I bet that baby is deep," whistled Jimmy.

"Yes," agreed Kiki, "very deep. Karl's motorcycle is in there."

"I wondered what happened to that bike. I guess the Germans are running so fast they didn't have time to stop and worry about Karl or his cycle."

Kiki and Jimmy ate their cheese and bread. Kiki had packed two bottles of wine.

"No wonder the damn knapsack was so heavy."

Kiki said she ran into Marie who told her Jacques had proposed marriage. Marie told him, "No." Things were just fine as they were.

Kiki smiled, "Maybe, Jacques is worried about some handsome man falling into Marie's life."

She looked at Jimmy, grinned, and asked, "Are you feeling strong, healed and healthy."

"I feel great thanks to you and Jacques, but especially you. I don't know if I have ever been healthier."

"That is good," she said.

"I heard that in England, people say of you Yank flyboys that you're 'overpaid, over-sexed and over here.' Is that true?"

"Is that true that is what the English say?"

Kiki laughed and punched his leg.

"No, is that truly how you handsome flyboys are?"

Jimmy looked into Kiki's lovely eyes and winked.

"Well, I am certainly not overpaid."

Kiki spread a large blanket on the meadow and started unbuttoning her dress.

"Hurry," she said, tugging at Jimmy's belt.

"But these are your late husband's pants."

"He won't mind. Take them off."

Afterwards, they lay in each other's arms. "Well, Mr. Flyboy, you have recovered very nicely, I must say."

"I had a good trainer. Very thorough."

The August sun was high in the sky. Kiki jumped up and said, "Let's swim."

She ran and dove headfirst. Jimmy, naked, stepped gingerly into the water.

"Sweet Jesus, it's freezing."

Kiki splashed Jimmy unmercifully and pulled him down into her arms. They swam for ten minutes. Kiki stood and strode from the lake. Jimmy watched her dash for a towel, all pink, sinew, and loveliness. She was a gift from God.

As she patted herself dry, Kiki smiled as Jimmy emerged from the water.

"Well, the lake might be cold but it seems a certain oversexed flyboy is back at attention."

"Once more into the breech," snarled Jimmy as he ran towards her.

From thence, Jimmy and Kiki slept together at the farmhouse. If Jacques cared, he said nothing. Just grinned at them each morning.

"You two sleep well last night? Creaking noises kept me awake."

Kiki said, "Jimmy is fit again. Now he must relearn to be a co-pilot. He is my beautiful co-pilot."

One night, afterwards, Jimmy whispered to Kiki, "And you think I am the one who is oversexed?'

She kissed him on the lips and said, "I am French."

On a clear morning in mid-September, at breakfast, Jacques said that the American and French Resistance forces would be rolling through the village that day as liberators. He and Marie would be joining in the celebration.

Jimmy and Kiki looked at one another. Jimmy sighed.

"We knew this day would come. I must rejoin them and return to England."

Kiki's beautiful eyes welled with tears. She knew he had to leave, just as her husband had four years earlier.

"I will put out your uniform. You want to look like the brave hero you are."

She ran from the kitchen.

Jimmy looked at Jacques, who shrugged and squeezed Jimmy's arm.

"Go say a proper farewell to my sister then we will all go into the village to greet our saviors."

In the village, advance units handed French and American flags to anyone with a hand. A uniformed Jimmy, Kiki, Jacques, and Marie stood on the roadside as the first French Resistance troops marched into the village.

In a jeep leading the parade stood Colonel Albert Eon.

"Well, I'll be damned."

The Colonel waved and saluted the crowd. He spotted Jimmy. A big grin lit up his otherwise dour visage. Eon stopped the parade, jumped from his jeep, and summoned Jimmy. Ensign Linker smartly saluted.

"Sir. Good to see you, sir."

"And it's damn good to see you again Ensign…Ensign??"

"Ensign James Linker, sir."

"I was told you and the other pilot had been killed. Never heard from again."

"Ensign Goeller, sir. Brave man. He held the plane steady while I bailed out. It blew up before he could jump. I've been hiding here waiting to see the good guys to come get me. Thank you for coming and so swiftly."

Like any Colonel, Eon lapped up praise.

Eon grabbed a Lieutenant, introduced him to Linker.

"Take this man to Rennes immediately and put him on the first plane back to England. We will stop here for the evening. Get Ensign Linker heading home now."

Jimmy saluted Colonel Eon again and told the Lieutenant to give him a minute. He returned and hugged Marie, hugged and shook Jacques's hand, then looked at Kiki.

In a trembling lip, she said, "I am impressed. You know our famous Colonel Eon."

"Yeah, I used to be his chauffeur. I am coming back, Kiki. I'm coming back when this is all over and get you. I love you."

Kiki cupped Jimmy's face in her hands.

"My brave, beautiful Angel Jimmy. Don't be so brave. Stay alive. Go home and make some lucky American girl happy, like you have made me happy. Promise me that you will survive. That is the only promise I want from you. Do you promise?"

"I promise." Jimmy squeezed her hand. She asked that he not kiss her goodbye in front of her neighbors. Their tongues chatter enough.

"Au revoir, Jimmy."

Ensign James Linker hopped into a jeep and was whisked away.

Chapter 5: Young Mr. Sorensen

Linker returned to Special Air Unit 1. He was placed in a hospital for a few days and released in good shape. Captain Green filed the necessary papers for Jimmy to be awarded several medals, including the Air Medal and a Purple Heart.

Jimmy thanked Captain Green, though he hardly cared about any of that.

Then Green dropped the bomb.

"Jimmy you're being transferred to the Pacific Theater immediately. This Aphrodite boondoggle is about finished. Complete failure. A super top-secret big failure so you can never disclose anything about it. Probably forever."

"Why the transfer, sir?"

"Two reasons, son. First, Aphrodite is about finished but it isn't fully finished. Those dumb bastards are liable to send a few more flying bombs on suicide missions before they admit they're wrong. I don't want you on one of those suicide missions."

Green calmly looked into Jimmy's eyes.

"Second, I've heard you have been making a nuisance of yourself about some French girl. Hell, Jimmy, half the GIs on the Continent think they've fallen in love with some French or Italian cupcake."

"With respect, sir, Kiki is not a cupcake?"

"Kiki? Look, Ensign, millions of beautiful, lovely, horny girls have been patiently waiting for you boys back home. I don't think they'd appreciate a bunch of war brides getting off those troop ships."

"I will find her, sir."

"Well, good luck finding her from Saipan. Dismissed."

In June, 1951, Jimmy Linker was supervising a bridge building unit for the State of Maine. He took a call from someone who introduced himself as Ted Sorensen. Linker would typically ignore such a call but he was ordered to speak to Sorensen by the Chairman of the Maine State Highway Commission. Sorensen wanted to meet for lunch.

"Is that okay with you?"

"My boss says it has to be okay with me." Linker agreed to meet Sorensen at the Augusta Country Club.

Ted Sorensen was a damn baby. Tall, thin, bespeckled, with a professorial demeanor way past his years. "Twenty-five, tops," thought Linker.

"Thank you, Mr. Linker, for meeting with me. Sorry to pull rank on you. My boss is a very insistent gentleman and people…powerful people…take his calls."

"What do you want with a small fry like me, Mr. Sorensen?"

Sorensen looked at a legal pad he had withdrawn from his briefcase.

"In August 1944, you were assigned to a top-secret Naval air group in England that was testing a remotely controlled flying bomb. That correct?"

"Well, if it's top-secret then I can't talk about it. Have a nice day, Mr. Sorensen." Linker rose from the table.

"Wait. You flew with Joe Kennedy. Joe Kennedy, Jr. I work for Joe Kennedy Sr. Just give me a few minutes to explain."

Sorensen put the legal pad in his briefcase.

Linker sat back down. "Go on."

"Joseph P. Kennedy is a very rich, powerful man, who is used to getting what he wants. The Navy has been stonewalling him for seven years about the circumstances surrounding Joe Jr.'s death."

"Joe was flying with a different guy that day. Not me. Or we would not be having this swell chat."

"Yeah, I know. Just tracking you down has been crazy. A fellow named Green, who had no more interest in talking to me than you do, off-handedly dropped your name."

"Well, that's funny."

"Look if you were Joe Jr.'s co-pilot you probably knew him pretty well. His father had big plans for him, as the eldest son. Joe Sr. was determined to get his namesake into the White House. Nothing less."

"I'm pretty sure Joe was aware of his father's ambitions for him. He joked about it."

"Now Joe's younger brother Jack is the anointed one. Senior still intends to get a son elected president. Jack will run for Senate next year against Henry Cabot Lodge, whose family is Mayflower blueblood with a well-established political pedigree."

Linker shrugged, 'Yeah?"

"My job is to create a legend, if you will, around the Kennedy clan. Make them look every bit as entitled to leadership as the Cabot Lodges. Turn these second-generation Irish immigrants into Brahmins."

Linker shrugged, "Good luck."

"A big part of this legend is going to be built on the war heroics of the Kennedy brothers. Jack was a big hero in the Pacific, well-documented. Joe was a hero too, a martyr, but no one knows the particulars. We can't be fools and claim something about Joe's death that isn't true."

Sorensen pounded the table lightly.

"Lodge sat on his privileged ass during the war, something the Kennedy boys could have done but didn't. If we oversell Joe's exploits, though, we run the risk of looking like Irish liars. The rub is that prick Lodge probably has the full file on Joe Jr."

Linker sat up and looked at Sorensen.

"Here's what I'll tell you about Joe, Jr. He was a fine pilot. I could not have found a better one. He died doing an incredibly brave thing. That the Navy to this day still stamps it top-secret is shameful. Joe had completed his required missions but volunteered for this project. He died. I should have died with him. He was a good man."

Sorensen dove in.

"Can't you tell me more about the actual specifics of the project and what happened that day. What went wrong. Was it Joe's fault?"

Sorensen had reignited the cooling embers of Jimmy Linker's wartime resentments. About many things, not just the bad treatment of Joe Kennedy.

"I'll tell you what, Mr. Sorensen, if you do something for me, maybe I'll remember somethings I swore to forget."

"Go on, Mr. Linker."

"I met a girl over there in Brittany. Kiki DeChambeau. Near Rennes. I have thought of her every day for the last seven years, like old man Kennedy obsessing about his boy. The Navy stonewalled me on my attempts to locate Kiki like they did you."

Now it was Linker's turn to stare intently at Sorensen.

"I went to Brittany and she and her family were gone. No one knew where. You find that girl for me, Mr. Sorensen, I don't care her circumstances, and I will be most grateful."

Sorensen smiled at Linker. He admired the romantic soul of the bridge builder. He nodded.

"I leave for England and France in two days. Let me see what I can do."

Both men stood and shook hands.

Three months later to the day, Jimmy Linker received a letter on personal, embossed stationary from Ted Sorensen:

Dear Mr. Linker:

Thank you again for your time in Augusta. As you requested, I did make both official and unofficial inquiries as to your Mme. DeChambeau.

Unfortunately, I found no record of her. I am sorry. I did so much want to assist you, and not just because of the project I have been pursuing. That issue is under control, and we will not need any more of your time.

Sincerely, Ted Sorensen

Chapter 6: Boston

On November 27, 1963, Jimmy Linker, now President of his own successful bridge contracting firm, received a call from Ted Sorensen. He took this call on his own insistence.

"Hello."

"Hello, Mr. Linker, This is Ted Sorensen. I don't know if you remember me."

"Mr. Sorensen, of course I remember you. You were a punk kid when we met long ago. You are famous now. I brag about having lunch with you. I am so sorry for the tragedy in your life. The tragedy in all our lives."

"Thank you, Mr. Linker. It is all unbelievable. Horrifying. The Kennedys seem cursed."

"They do indeed, sir. They do indeed."

"Mr. Linker, the reason I am calling is to again prevail upon you for a favor."

"Anything, Mr. Sorensen. I promise not to be a horse's ass this time."

"I'll try to keep the same vow. A French politician named Alfred Eon accompanied Charles De Gaulle to the President's funeral."

"Colonel Eon?"

"I think he retired as a General. But, yes, the same. He is apparently writing a book about his wartime experiences and is using his time in the States to interview Americans with whom he crossed paths back in the day. And up popped your name."

"Well, we hardly shared much experience during the war."

"Nevertheless, he'd love to remake your acquaintance. He is at the Newbury in Boston. The State Department would consider it a great favor if you'd call on General Eon either tomorrow or Thursday. We can send a plane to Augusta to fetch you."

"That won't be necessary, sir. I'm a pilot, remember? I'll fly down to Logan tomorrow and shoot over to the Newbury by, say, 2:00pm."

"Mr. Linker, that would be marvelous. Please send us a bill for all your out-of-pocket expenses. I will let General Eon's people know."

The next day, at two, Jimmy Linker was welcomed into the Newbury VIP suite by Albert Eon. Still all nose and grandeur, he shook Jimmy's hand and bade him to sit. They talked for over an hour.

The General's recollection of being ferried to Brittany was scrambled. He believed he had parachuted in at night and was disappointed that his entrance was not quite as heroic. He had no recollection of meeting Jimmy again in the village.

Finally, Jimmy said, "Well good luck sir with your book. Sorry you had to come to America for such a sad reason. It was a pleasure seeing you again."

"Thank you, my boy. Oops, there's my family."

Two teenagers, a boy, and a girl, came into the suite with Mrs. Eon.

The boy was a good-looking kid who fortunately had not inherited his father's nose. His younger sister was going to be a stunner. Mrs. Eon, Kiki, had hardly changed at all.

Kiki looked at Jimmy and smiled a little sad smile.

"Darling, this is Ensign Linker who I knew back in the war. He was helping me with some research. Mr. Linker, this is my wife Kiki, our son Jacques, and our daughter Bridget."

Jimmy tried hard not to stare at Kiki. He failed. After an awkward silence, Jimmy spoke.

"Well, thank you General for your hospitality. Sorry, again, for the sad circumstances of your visit."

"You're welcome. Yes, the last few days have been especially sad for Kiki. She and Mrs. Kennedy have become good friends. Jackie always stops around whenever she's in Paris."

Bridget rolled her eyes.

"Nice meeting you all. Godspeed."

James Linker rode an elevator to the lobby, used the men's room, stepped outside, and asked a doorman to hail a cab to Logan.

"Jimmy, wait."

He turned and said, "Kiki, you are as lovely as the day we met."

"Jimmy, please, one coffee in the Lobby. Five minutes."

He knew he was about to have his heart ripped out. He returned to the hotel lobby and sat with Kiki at a small table by a window.

"I had no idea you would be here today. I asked Albert why you had visited and he said Ted Sorensen thought it might be a good idea for Albert's book. Albert has no recollection of you so I'm not sure what Ted was thinking. That book, by the way, he has been writing since 1945."

She attempted to smile, with little success.

"I tried to find you."

"The day you left, Albert invited several of us to join him for dinner. I was heartbroken and didn't want to go. But I did. Then a few weeks later, he came back to the village looking for me and …life happens."

Jimmy looked at Kiki and smiled.

"Kiki, I am just glad that you are alive and happy and hanging out with Jackie Kennedy. Life happens and I am glad for you. Your daughter is beautiful, and your son is very handsome too. Is he named after your brother? How is Jacques anyway?"

Kiki smiled at Jimmy and shook her head.

"Jacques is fine. Lives in Marseille with Marie and five kids. But my son, Jimmy, is named after his father, not my brother."

Kiki squeezed Jimmy's hand.

"I was pregnant when Albert came calling. He knew it. I told him the father was a soldier. Albert didn't care. He has raised Jacques as his own son. Loves him as his own son. And Jacques loves him."

"I would never interfere with that."

"I know, Jimmy. In a few years Jacques is going to look just like my Jimmy. It will be so bittersweet for me. But we French love bittersweet. I must get back upstairs now."

Kiki stood and bent to kiss Jimmy one last time. He smiled and held her hand.

"Thank you, Kiki, for peeking."

"Mon plaisir, Monsieur." And she was gone, into the lobby crowd.

Epilogue

Jimmy taxied to Harvard Square. He sat on a bench and nursed a coffee from a street vendor. The crowd was subdued, no doubt on account of the sad days since Friday.

Jimmy spoke to himself.

"Linker, you jackass. You have been wasting your life chasing an empty fantasy. You have been missing, Linker, since you got home from that goddamn war. Green was right, America is full of lovely, smart, horny girls. You don't need some French cupcake."

Across the quadrant sat a petite, curly-haired, woman reading a giant hardback book. Jim smiled to himself, shrugged, and walked over to the girl.

"Hi there, what're you reading?"

"A book." She smiled.

"Is it one I would like?"

"Do you like Criminal Justice Theory?"

'Um…I love it. What do you think of bridge builders?"

She carefully marked her place and closed her book.

"Hello, I'm Carol. I adore bridge builders."

Jimmy laughed, "Hi…I am Jimmy…the bridge builder."

Meet the Author

Jon Ketzner was born in Cumberland, Maryland in the lovely Appalachian foothills. He grew up in Baltimore then graduated from Towson University with a degree in mathematics and went on to a long career as a consulting actuary. For many years, Jon and his family lived in Bryn Mawr, Pennsylvania before moving back to Cumberland in 1990.

As a recovering actuary and inspired by the Maryland Writers Association's "Notable Authors" monthly challenges, Jon decided to try his hand at writing and give his left-brain side a rest. He cites as influences: Henry Fielding, Joseph Heller, Gregory McDonald, and Tim Dorsey.

Made in the USA
Middletown, DE
17 May 2023

30740964R00161